CAPITALIZING ON LOVE

A Sweet Romance

Billionaire's Bet

Book 5

A.B. PROEBSTEL

ISBN-13: 978-1-946292-40-7

ISBN-10: 1-946292-40-0

Printed in the United States of America

First Printing, 2021

Second Printing, 2023

Website: https://geni.us/LOA-Home
BookBub: https://geni.us/BBFollow
Goodreads: www.goodreads.com/aproebstel
Facebook: https://geni.us/FB-LOA
X: https://geni.us/Amy-T
Instagram: www.instagram.com/amyproebstel

BOOKS IN THE BILLIONAIRE'S BET SERIES

Book Zero: A Billionaire's Patent for Love

Book One: A Cowboy's Recipe for Romance

Book Two: Loving Texas Tea

Book Three: Properties of Love

Book Four: Plane Love

Book Five: Capitalizing on Love

Book Six: An Unleashed Love

Book Seven: Ether of Love

DEDICATION

First of all, this book is dedicated to my friends and family. Your support in helping me carve out time to write and your encouragement to keep me going even when life got in the way, has been utterly amazing. I've been so inspired by your thoughtfulness and I hope it shows in my writing.

Secondly, to the readers of this series, I greatly appreciate all of your kind words, amazing reviews, and support along the way. None of this would be possible without your enthusiasm for the characters and their stories.

CHAPTER 1

MARKSON

"**B**race for impact!"

Markson's heart raced as he uttered the chilling words he never thought he'd have to say.

The once-tranquil flight had turned into a nightmare as his almost-new private jet's engine exploded, leaving them hurtling toward the ground over the majestic Great Smoky Mountains.

With a determined grip on the yoke, Markson fought to maintain control of the plummeting aircraft. He prayed for a miracle as he aimed them toward a small clearing surrounded by dense trees. It was their only chance of survival, but he knew it would be a perilous endeavor.

Branches snapped against the wingtips, but Markson's focus remained unwavering. He added every ounce of flight input he could muster, trying to eke out any extra distance.

His heart pounded in his chest, and sweat dripped down his forehead as the ground rushed to meet them.

The landing gear hit the forest floor with a bone-jarring impact, shaking the cabin violently, worse than his practice landings from ten years ago when he first learned to fly. Markson's hands were numb from the tension, yet he couldn't afford to relax just yet.

Turning his attention to his lone passenger, he searched for any signs of injury. Her eyes met his, wide with shock, but she seemed surprisingly composed. Markson felt a wave of relief wash over him as she appeared unharmed. He didn't want to face his worst nightmare of someone dying because of his flying.

He unstrapped himself from his seat. "Are you alright?" he asked, his voice still trembling with adrenaline.

Her wide-eyed stare caught his. It appeared as though she'd watched him this whole time. One of her hands pressed against the cockpit ceiling, and the other clutched the edge of her seat. She appeared fine, and Markson sighed, relieved to escape their imminent danger seemingly unscathed.

As the adrenaline surged through Markson's veins, he focused on his passenger, who seemed dazed and confused after the crash. "Nichole, talk to me. Are you hurt?" he asked, his voice urgent and concerned.

Her eyes remained unfocused as she shook her head, her hair flying wildly around her. "I think I'm fine. What happened? How is the airplane still intact after losing the engine?" she asked, her voice shaky and shrill.

Relieved that she was at least coherent, Markson explained, "I pulled the parachute."

Nichole looked at him skeptically. "That's not funny, Mark. Planes don't have parachutes," she protested.

Ignoring her disbelief, Markson continued, "This one does."

He grabbed the emergency landing card and began systematically following the steps for complete shutdown and evacuation. "Unbuckle; we need to exit the plane." Markson felt terrible about his unfeeling tone and looked over to his passenger, hoping to look reassuring but intent on having his instructions followed immediately.

Fear crept into Nichole's eyes. "Exit? Why? Isn't it better to stay with the wreckage until help arrives?" she asked.

Markson shook his head. "Not if the airplane catches on fire. We won't know if it's safe until we inspect the fuselage.

Until then, we're going outside. Luckily, it's still daylight," he insisted, his tone firm and urgent.

Nichole hesitated for a moment, but Markson's intent gaze and urgent voice convinced her. With trembling hands, she unbuckled her seatbelt before her gaze shifted to the darkening view beyond the windshield. "Barely. How long do you think it'll take for someone to rescue us?" she said, her voice determined.

Markson wasted no time. With practiced efficiency, he guided Nichole toward the exit.

As they stepped into the cabin, Markson scanned for smoke or damage, ensuring there were no immediate dangers. "We'll have to spend the night inside the airplane. It'll take a couple of hours for rescue teams to find us," he explained.

Markson cursed himself for putting Nichole through this ordeal. She shouldn't have been on this flight in the first place. If it weren't for his friend's favor, he wouldn't have flown this ill-fated path to Gatlinburg with her.

When he first saw Nichole's beauty, suspicion gnawed at him. Was this another attempt to set him up?

But her reason for traveling on short notice changed his mind. He understood the desperation she felt; he would have done the same if one of his parents became sick enough to require hospitalization.

Leading the way to the main cabin door, Markson opened a compartment and retrieved the emergency supply bag. Unlocking the exterior door, he pushed it open with a sense of relief. It could have easily been jammed shut by the impact or debris, but luck was on their side.

He quickly descended the steps and extended his hand to help Nichole out of the airplane. Her hand felt delicate and cold, and he couldn't help but notice her composure despite the terrifying situation they found themselves in.

Part of him wanted to take a moment to hold her, to provide comfort in the midst of chaos, but he knew it was inappropriate. They were not friends, barely acquaintances, yet they now shared this harrowing experience.

As Nichole stood in front of him, he hesitated, indecision making him feel awkward. Markson gazed into her eyes, feeling a connection that went beyond words.

She cleared her throat, and he stepped back, refocusing on the task at hand. There was a job to finish, and she seemed composed enough not to need his immediate support.

Still, the desire to offer comfort through a hug lingered in Markson's mind. He fought the urge, knowing that in this moment of crisis, his priority was their safety. As they stood together amidst the wreckage, the bond of this shared experience created an unspoken understanding between them.

Scanning their surroundings, Markson couldn't help but whistle in awe at their stroke of luck with the landing. The densely packed trees surrounded them, their branches broken in places, showing just how narrowly they had escaped a much worse fate. Recovering the airplane would be a challenge for later; right now, their priority was survival.

Unbelievably, the jet was intact with only a few wingtip scratches and a deployed chute. He turned to Nichole, his heart still racing from the adrenaline-fueled descent. "I think I just used up six of my nine lives. We were incredibly lucky, you know?" He expected a response, but when she remained silent, he noticed her frustration as she fiddled with her cell phone.

After a slight pause, she replied, "Yeah, but I'll feel better about all of this once I can make sure my dad is okay as well. Ugh! Can I use your cell phone? Mine doesn't have any service, and the battery is getting low."

"Of course. Let's see if we can get a signal." Markson passed her his phone, his hands trembling slightly from the aftermath of their harrowing landing. He unlocked it with a swipe and watched as she tried to find a signal, her expression fraught with concern.

Guilt washed over him; he should have offered his phone sooner. He had to stay strong and in charge for as long as it took to get Nichole to civilization.

"Everything checks out," he said, picking up the emergency bag. "Why don't we go back inside the airplane to wait for help?"

Nichole turned, and in a flash, her expression shifted from compliant eagerness to fear. He knew that look all too well, the same one he saw when he called out the first mayday. His instincts kicked in, and he positioned himself protectively between her and whatever danger lurked behind them.

The cracking of twigs amplified his senses. Markson tensed, turning to face whatever threat approached.

As the man neared them with a rifle in hand, Markson's heart pounded in his chest.

"Thank goodness. We thought we'd have to wait for hours. How did you find us so fast?" Markson called out, attempting to remain composed.

The man stepped into a patch of sunlight, his grip on the rifle tightening. His expression was anything but friendly, and

Markson's instincts screamed danger. "I'll be the one asking questions here, mister," the man retorted coldly. "How many others are on board?"

Relief quickly turned to dread as the man's hostile demeanor became apparent. This wasn't the help they were hoping for; they had stumbled upon something far more dangerous.

Markson tried to reason with the man, his hands raised in surrender, making the emergency bag strap slip up to his elbow. "None. It's just the two of us. Look, if you have a landline, we can call for help and be on our way."

"Shut up! I know about your tricks. I'm not stupid, you know!" the man snapped, his eyes wild. "You and your partner can start marching around your chopper and toward my cabin. I don't know how you found me, but I won't be retaken. Never again will I let that happen. Do you understand me? Get moving!" He lifted the rifle until the barrel pointed vaguely in their direction.

Markson's mind raced for a way to handle the situation. He didn't want to risk any sudden moves that might set the man off. Slowly backing away, he kept his arm protectively around Nichole, shielding her from the man's line of sight.

Even in the worst parts of Atlanta, he'd never felt this helpless. He had to do something to control this situation before anything happened to either of them.

He took several cautious steps backward. "This guy's off his rocker," Markson whispered to Nichole, careful not to move his lips. "We have to run before we get to his cabin. There's no telling what he'd do to us if he got us inside. As soon as we get around the airplane, I want you to start running as fast as you can. I'll bring up the rear to protect you. No matter what happens, keep running. Got it?"

With a barely noticeable nod, Nichole signaled her understanding. Her eyes darted between Markson and the approaching man. She stayed close to his side. Markson was relieved by her composed response to the dire situation. In his past experiences, the women he'd known would have succumbed to hysteria in such circumstances. Not Nichole. She remained surprisingly poised.

He swiftly slung the emergency pack behind him, securing it with the straps. They couldn't afford to leave their survival gear behind. Markson felt a sense of reassurance having it with him, even if it offered little real protection against their pursuer.

Checking Nichole's footwear, he was relieved to find her wearing sturdy laced tennis shoes. The thought of her complaining about designer shoes in this perilous situation would have been too much to handle. With proper footwear, they stood a better chance of navigating the treacherous terrain ahead.

Despite the danger they faced, Markson couldn't help but feel a glimmer of hope. If they moved quickly and took advantage of the cover of darkness, they might be able to outmaneuver the deranged man hunting them down.

Leaving the crash site behind was difficult, but they had no other choice. Their priority was to escape and then figure out their next move. Markson urged Nichole to go faster, and she complied, proving to be remarkably quick and agile. He admired her capability and determination; she was better equipped for this situation than he had expected.

As they reached the cover of the nearby jet, Markson gently pushed against Nichole's back, encouraging her to keep moving. She responded swiftly, showing her readiness to face this challenging escape. She shot away from him even though he'd barely touched her. She'd followed his instruction to a tee. Man, that girl was fast. Thank goodness.

Markson kept his promise to stay one step behind Nichole, lengthening his stride to match her pace. They weaved through the first few trees at the edge of the clearing, navigating the rough terrain with determination. But their progress didn't go unnoticed; the deranged man's angry shouts echoed behind them, driving them to push even harder.

As they hurried through the dense forest, Markson couldn't help but wonder what had driven the man to see them as a threat. It became evident that he had likely experienced captivity in the past, possibly as a prisoner of war during the Vietnam War. The man's reference to their jet as a "chopper" reinforced this suspicion. Markson knew they had to be cautious; there was no telling what lengths the man would go to avoid being recaptured.

Nichole's agile movements kept them on course, swiftly dodging through the forest like a seasoned survivor. She had the grace of a deer. But Markson couldn't fully appreciate it as their lives hung in the balance.

A sudden gunshot pierced the air, and Nichole made a sharp turn to the left.

Markson stumbled over a tree root, pain shooting through his body as he crashed hard onto the ground. He fought to catch his breath, debris falling around him as he struggled to rise.

Determined not to be left behind, he pushed himself up and forced his aching muscles to keep moving.

Markson's momentary doubt about the gun being loaded vanished like wisps of smoke in a stiff breeze. He knew that split-second stumble had saved him from the gunshot.

The reality of the situation hit him like a ton of bricks – this man was willing to kill to ensure his freedom. The gravity of the danger they were in weighed heavily on Markson's mind.

His life and Nichole's were now at the mercy of a deranged stranger.

Could this day get any worse?

Maybe.

He shouldn't tempt fate.

As they ran, Markson couldn't help but worry about being separated from Nichole. It was a risk he couldn't afford to take. He pushed his body to its limits, closing the distance between them. The thought of losing her and being left alone in this perilous situation haunted him.

In the chaos of their escape, Markson also realized that Nichole still had his cell phone. It was their only hope of getting rescued from this remote wilderness. The urgency to reach her and retrieve the phone fueled his determination to keep up the pace.

With the pursuit still on their tail, they raced through the unforgiving wilderness, hoping that fate would favor them.

CHAPTER 2
NICHOLE

Racing through the woods didn't have the same pleasure as it had when she was a child. Terror added extra length to her strides while she leaped over another rotting log. How had this day gotten so bad?

Her problems whirled through her mind as fast as her feet passed over the forest floor. She desperately needed to get to her father's side at the hospital. If anything happened to him, she wasn't sure she could ever forgive herself. If only she'd had the patience to wait for the commercial flight scheduled for the next morning, she wouldn't be in this mess. Her friend's offer of a private flight had seemed too good to be true. Now she knew it was.

Why was fate being so cruel to her? This trip should have been a simple, twenty-seven-minute flight. Even now, she should be in a rental car, heading to the hospital. But no, she was dodging bullets from some lunatic hermit in the

Great Smoky Mountains—as if surviving a plane crash wasn't nearly enough of a distraction or delay.

Once they made it back to civilization, she'd have some choice words for her friend for setting up this flight. In her rush to get to her father's hospital bedside, she hadn't given any thought to the pilot's proficiency or the soundness of the airplane. Granted, she always assumed private jets were meticulously maintained, but now she knew better.

Thankfully, the route she chose to run was mostly downhill. Her fortuitous choice of shoes helped tremendously in keeping her footing over the uneven terrain. When she heard the first gunshot striking the tree, she'd had a momentary bout of panic, mostly when Mark fell at the same time. She thought he might have been hit, but then she'd heard him continue his run behind her.

She slowed her pace to allow him to catch up. Even though these woods were familiar territory to her, she didn't relish the idea of being alone or of being responsible for the pilot getting hopelessly lost. She doubted he had much practical experience in wilderness survival. Even though he had a great body, it probably came from working out in a fancy gym in Atlanta rather than roughing it in the Smoky Mountains woods.

The second shot sounded much too far away to have any accuracy. The crazy hermit probably wanted them to keep running. At this point, she didn't mind complying. The idea of resting anywhere near that man made her want to renew her original pace to put more distance between them.

"Hey! I think we've gone far enough," Mark shouted from pretty far behind her.

His stamina had surprised her. For a city man, he had done remarkably well. Wishing she could pretend to ignore him, she took several more steps before coming to a complete stop. With her hands on her hips, she turned and waited for him to catch up.

She couldn't restrain her lips from curling up at the sight of him. He wasn't nearly as coordinated as she had imagined. But he had kept up with her, which did give him some points for his effort. He took the last few steps to reach her, bent over with his hands resting above his knees, and gulped for air. With flushed cheeks, he looked like he was ready to pass out.

"Are you okay?" she asked.

"Just winded," he managed to answer between gasps for breath. "You're fast."

"That's what I get for training to be the national junior Olympic cross country champion. I'm glad I still have it." She couldn't help but blush at his praise. More than one boyfriend had dumped her because of her love for the sport. Plus, she really didn't have time to spend with them since all of her spare time went into running practice.

Mark nodded, his body finally straightened, but his chest still billowed. He glanced behind them, obviously nervous.

"I don't think we have to worry about him. Besides, the birds would warn us long before he got near." She looked around, hoping to find any landmarks which might help them discover their new location. The phone, still clutched in her hand, buzzed with an incoming message.

"Oh! I never did get a chance to see if your phone had service. I think it does!" She glanced down at the screen, which displayed an unread text message. She hadn't meant to snoop, but she read it all the same. "Who was the hot babe?" it read.

More than a little embarrassed, she shoved the phone into his outstretched hand. Turning her back, she pulled out her phone again. The screen didn't even light up anymore with the motion—the battery must have drained completely. Their last hope lay in Mark's cell.

"Can you hear me?" Mark practically yelled into his phone.

Nichole turned to watch. Mark held the phone up, shifting position to gain any new angle which might help with reception. Her experience with these mountains was that they would have to be extremely lucky to get a call to go through. Even receiving that one text might have been a minor miracle.

"You're wasting your time, Mark. We'll just have to keep walking until we get to a forest trail. Save your battery for when we have better reception."

She wearily sighed as Mark continued striking new poses with the phone held high. How long could he keep this up? Why did men always have to be so stubborn?

She couldn't take it anymore. Rather than continue to grow frustrated with him, she turned to survey their surroundings. The land sloped down; the trees leaned from the wind blowing through the hollow. Inhaling, she felt herself relax. This was home, the world in which she'd grown up.

Now, all she had to do was read the land enough to get them back to civilization. Unlike most people thrown into this situation, she didn't worry; she knew this landscape. She'd spent her childhood roaming through the countryside, maybe even this very spot. Closing her eyes, she concentrated on the breeze, the sounds of the wildlife, and the warmth of the sun on her face.

Turning slowly to her left, she knew where to go. But their journey wouldn't be easy, nor would it be quick. Her sense of direction always impressed her father, but thinking of him made her heart race. Would she make it back to Gatlinburg in time? Was he still fighting for his life in the hospital?

"Penny for your thoughts," Mark said, his shoulder brushing against hers as he came to a stop beside her. "Hey, are you okay? I mean, I know we're lost, but I'm sure we can find someone not as crazy as that guy," he flapped his hand behind them, "to help us."

She hated that he'd seen her moment of pain and weakness. Nobody saw the part of her; she usually kept a firm grip on her emotions. Her nursing career ensured she didn't let people see what she really thought. But she'd slipped; she'd left herself open. And Mark had called her out on it.

Squaring her shoulders, she felt the mask of professionalism drop over her expression. Turning, she looked up at Mark and said, "I'm not lost. We just have a long way to go before we can reach help."

Mark's lips curled up, and a small guffaw escaped from his mouth. He crossed his arms over his chiseled chest, emphasizing her initial impression of too many hours spent in a gym. "Not lost—are you sure you didn't hit your head in the crash? Of course, we're lost. Unless you can say, you've actually been in this spot before, which I seriously doubt since we're literally in the middle of nowhere."

"Whatever!" Nichole turned on her heel. She didn't need to explain anything to this guy. Besides, once they reached a place with cell service and rescuers arrived, she'd never set eyes on him again. Nothing could be gained by standing still; besides, her nerves insisted on her staying active. "Let's keep walking until you've caught your breath again. I have someplace I need to be."

Markson immediately caught up with her. His pace exactly matched hers. "What did they tell you about your dad's condition?"

Nichole took several more steps before she decided to answer him. It wasn't in her to be rude, and he was trying to make conversation. Maybe that was his way to calm himself. After all, he was the one who was lost.

She stared straight ahead, her voice coming out calm and even. "My dad was actually the one who called me. He said he was experiencing chest pain and thought maybe he should go to the emergency room to get checked out."

"That doesn't sound so bad. It doesn't mean he's actually in danger. Did he drive himself or call for an ambulance?"

"Of course, he drove himself. But you don't know my dad. He hates hospitals; he never complains about anything. Good grief, he almost cut off two of his fingers with a circular saw, and he didn't even want to go to the doctor to get stitches."

"Maybe he didn't need them."

Nichole rolled her eyes, trying to regain her patience. "Mark, I could see his bones. He definitely needed stitches. Fourteen of them, to be exact. And that was after I practically pushed him into my car and drove him myself to the doctor. If I'd had lidocaine, he would have asked me to do the sutures just to avoid the doctors."

"Really?"

"Really, what?"

"Could you have stitched him up yourself?"

Sighing, she said, "I should be offended at your lack of faith in my ability. But you don't know me, so I'll let you off this time. Yes, I could've done it. I'm a registered nurse."

"No way. Seriously? You totally don't look the part."

She stopped in her tracks, turned, and crossed her arms defensively. She didn't even notice that she'd struck the same pose Mark had earlier until his eyebrow rose and his eyes shifted to register her stance. Immediately, she dropped her arms, balling her fists at her sides to contain her frustration at him. "What in the world is that supposed to mean? What does a nurse look like where you're from?"

Another eyebrow lifted before he grinned and answered, "I don't know. Old, ugly, and crotchety. Nothing at all like you. I would've said you were a model or maybe an actress."

She didn't want to dwell on the second part of his comment about her looks. Her genetics shouldn't factor into her chosen career, but it had always made her job more difficult. The doctors usually treated her like she was too pretty to have any brains. But then, the other nurses didn't like her because they were jealous of the doctors' attention to her because of it.

"Wow, you've just managed to offend the entire world of hardworking nurses. Why would you think such a thing?"

Color rushed into his cheeks, and he had the decency to look away. "Probably because it described the only nurse I spent much time with who worked at my high school. She hated football and thought it was a waste of her time tending to our injuries. She was all of the things I said, plus I swear she purposely made the treatment hurt worse than the initial injury. I think she got some sick pleasure from it."

"Well, I guess I could understand why you'd feel that way. Sorry I jumped all over you. I guess it touched a nerve with me." Resuming her walking, she added, "My dad didn't want me to go into nursing. He wanted me to work for the family company."

Why had she said all of that? He didn't need to know her personal business. Before he could get any ideas that she wanted to continue talking about herself, she changed tactics. "So, you played football in high school, huh? What position?"

"Quarterback."

Nichole rolled her eyes and chuckled. "Figures."

"What's that supposed to mean?"

She purposely looked him up and down before replying. "Because you're tall, well-built, and good-looking. Plus, you're pretty fast when someone is shooting at you. Although you could work on your coordination. Just saying."

"Ah, so you think I'm good-looking, huh?"

"Of course, that's the only part you heard—typical man. I'm not going to play into your ego. I'm sure you get enough of that from all the women throwing themselves at you." She grinned at him but noticed his smile faltered at the last part of her statement. Was it possible he had the same problem with his looks as she'd experienced?

"I'm sorry. That was rude for me to say." She should have kept her mouth shut, but he seemed to push her buttons on purpose. "Did you play football in college?"

"Yep, full scholarship because of it."

"Were you one of those guys who thought you'd make a career out of it?"

"Of course. Almost every guy on the team dreams of that outcome."

She snorted, shaking her head at his foolishness. "How did that turn out? I hope you got good grades."

"Four-point-oh. I'd say it all worked out. I got into the first-round draft pick."

Nichole's eyes darted over to his. Had she heard him correctly? "For the NFL?"

Mark's head tilted back, and he laughed until his voice echoed back through the mountains to them.

Nichole grabbed his arm, squeezing hard in her urgency, and pulling at him until he stopped walking. "Shut up! Did you forget about the gunman chasing us?" She slowly turned her head, listening for any new signs of life coming toward them.

Mark's mouth snapped shut, and he looked down on her with narrowed eyes. "I thought you said the forest animals would let us know if he got close. Or were you just kidding?"

"No, I wasn't kidding. But who could hear anything over your cackling?" In a quieter voice, she said, "Are you going to answer my question?"

CHAPTER 3

MARKSON

"Well, it wasn't the NBA. Of course, it was the NFL. Should I be offended that you didn't think I'd get drafted?" Markson couldn't help teasing her. She made it so easy, and her reactions were priceless. Given that her job would naturally make her more polite, the fact that she was so prickly with him only furthered his opinion that she was scared for her father.

She turned away, suddenly acting shy. When she started walking, Markson stayed beside her. With a sideways glance, her eyes looked softer, more friendly when she said, "Okay, I totally deserved that. You know, I think we've gotten off to a pretty rough start. Why don't we start fresh from this point on?"

She sure was beautiful when she flashed her bright smile up to him. It was hard for him to think of anything other than agreeing with her. Something about her made him want to agree to anything she asked. He almost felt bewitched by her. That sounded stupid, even in the privacy of his thoughts. But still...there was something different about her than the girls who literally threw themselves at him.

Nichole had no idea how accurate her offhanded comment had been earlier. He didn't trust pretty women; they always had an agenda when it came to him. They didn't care about him as much as they cared about his money. He'd learned that the hard way. But he *did* learn. He wasn't about to make that mistake again.

He kept glancing toward her, hoping to keep his scrutiny to himself. His first opinions of her had been way off, much to his surprise. Even now, her sure steps and take-charge attitude was a welcome difference to the flighty and desperate girls who usually threw themselves at him. Heck, Nichole didn't even seem to like him, which was strangely attractive.

As it seemed they would be spending a few hours alone together, he decided to use this opportunity to get to know her a little better. It wasn't lost on him how she offered tidbits about herself before clamming up and deflecting the conversation back to himself. Maybe if he did offer to share more about himself, she would reciprocate.

He cleared his throat, sounding loud in the otherwise silent dark woods. Modulating his voice in an abundance of caution, he said, "Back to your question. Yes, I played for the NFL." He almost cringed with the memory.

"Wow. That must have been exciting. Who did you play for?" Nichole's demeanor changed; she looked up at him with a genuine smile and real interest.

Her sudden mood change set him on alert. "Are you a football fan?"

"Not at all, but I can appreciate the athleticism of it."

He nodded; her answer made sense. Markson replied, "The way the draft works is that the worst team in the NFL gets the first pick of the players who make the cut. Unfortunately, I made it into the first round draft, and the Miami Dolphins chose me."

"Oh! I had no idea. That doesn't seem very fair to the players. Couldn't you get traded?"

"They can, but it didn't happen for me. I played for the Dolphins." That admission still rankled. If only he could have played for a better team, then maybe he could have had a longer career without all of the pain.

"If you had a choice, where did you want to play?"

He hadn't really given that much thought. Taking a few seconds to consider, he answered, "Probably for the Dallas Cowboys. I've always liked them."

"Are you sure it wasn't because of their cheerleaders?" Nichole quirked an eyebrow playfully.

She had a point. "Well, they are pretty amazing. You have to agree with me there." He grinned when she refused to take the bait he'd dangled so temptingly in front of her. He'd have to try harder.

"Hmph." Her steps lengthened marginally as the downward slope steepened, yet she didn't lose any of her grace. "Well, you appear to have changed careers. How did you go from being a quarterback in the NFL to a corporate pilot?"

Markson's footing chose that moment to fail him. Flailing his arms, he barely managed to keep himself from an uncontrolled slide down the hill. Unfortunately, his hand didn't fare as well since he used it to grab some nearby brush and received several rips in his palm for his trouble.

Hissing, he inspected the damage, seeing the blood instantly pool into his cupped palm. "Man, that stings!" Thankfully, the darkness of the densely-wooded forest gave him enough privacy to hide the unbidden tears that sprang to his eyes. He hadn't felt this kind of intense pain in a very long time. And it didn't seem very manly to complain about or cry over a seemingly superficial scratch on his hand.

"Let me see that," Nichole said, her take-charge tone receiving his instant compliance. She tipped his hand from side to side, her fingers delicately prodding at his flesh. "Hmm. It's hard to see much in this light, but you tore yourself up pretty good based on the amount of blood pooling. There's a stream just ahead, we should rinse it out, and I can find some moss to pack over it until it stops bleeding."

Markson nodded, not realizing she couldn't see it, withdrawing his hand from hers and wishing he could divorce himself from the pains now shooting up his arm. How could this hurt so badly? Within minutes, they arrived at the rushing water, hardly what he'd call a stream. It looked more like a turbulent river to him.

Markson jumped onto a flat rock protruding partway into the roiling water with only an eye for getting pain relief. Kneeling, he bent over and plunged his offending hand into the icy water. He hadn't expected it to be quite so cold, but he couldn't complain about the instant relief it gave him. Within seconds, he lost all feeling to his extremity.

With fewer trees overhead, he had dim light to see. Pulling his hand out of the water, he inspected the damage. The intense cold made his skin almost white, outlining the damage with stark contrast. The jagged tear went through several layers; one spot near the center seemed especially deep. He'd been so preoccupied scrutinizing his hand; he hadn't noticed Nichole left him alone.

With a gentle touch on his shoulder, Nichole kneeled next to him, her thigh brushing against his. She briefly plunged her hand into the water and withdrew it. Opening her fist, she revealed a handful of wet moss. "Hold onto this until the pain stops. I should have warned you about the unstable footing. I'm sorry."

"It's not your fault I wasn't paying attention in the dark. Hey! How did you know there was a stream? Have you been here before? I thought you were kidding earlier, but now I'm not so sure." Markson curled his fingers over the dripping moss. He'd thought the plant would feel scratchy, but it was soothing and soft.

Nichole busied herself with rinsing her hands in the rushing water. She didn't look up as she answered, "It's hard to tell for sure, but I grew up playing in these woods. After a while, you get good at reading the land and knowing what to look and listen for."

Cupping her hands together, she scooped up the cold water and noisily slurped it. Sighing, she dropped the remaining drops and flicked her hands to remove the excess moisture. "I've missed all of this."

Markson's gaze remained riveted to her actions. Seeing her in her element transformed her. No longer was she merely an attractive female specimen; she radiated contentment, unlike anything he'd ever witnessed before. Feeling as though he were an unwelcome voyeur, he mumbled, "I should see if there's cell reception here."

Belatedly, he remembered that he'd put his phone in his front pants pocket. With his injured hand, it would be awkward to retrieve it.

Nichole stood, shaking her head and surveying their surroundings. "Don't bother. It won't work down in this hollow. We'll have to wait until we get into a meadow or on top of the next ridge before we'll have any chance at all."

Markson stood abruptly, heedless of the proximity of his footing to the edge of the water. He hadn't realized how little space the rock offered for two adults; his chest brushed against

Nichole's arm as he rose. He lost his balance and teetered precariously.

Nichole's hand grabbed his bicep, pulling him toward her as she stepped back onto the rocky slope. He hadn't expected such strength in her, nor was he prepared for the sudden move forward. His whole body crashed against her, but she stood her ground, even as the breath rushed from her lungs. "Be careful, Mark. Jeesh! Don't you have any self-preservation?"

Markson wasn't thinking about any of that. "Sorry. You said next ridge. Just how far do you think we'll have to go before we can reach someone to help us?" He wasn't precisely panicked, but he didn't relish the idea of spending the night in the woods, especially with that gun-wielding man somewhere out there.

Her palms rested against his chest, and her voice came out almost breathlessly, "You don't know much about these mountains, do you?"

Only then did Markson realize their position. Not that he minded having her touch him, but this wasn't a good time to see where things could go. A grin pulled at the side of his mouth at the same time as he flexed his pecks. "Do you approve?"

Just as he expected, she pulled away as though she'd burned herself. Her complexion turned rosy, and she balled her hands at her sides. "I should have let you fall in the creek. Maybe then, you'd be cooling your jets instead of making moves on me."

"Hey, I wasn't the one with my hands all over you." She glared up at him before turning sharply away from him. To her back, he called out, " Just saying."

Without another word, she stomped away. He hoped it was in the right direction. As far as he was concerned, it all looked the same around them. He chuckled as he jogged to catch up with her.

"Truce, okay?" he offered.

"Fine."

Her tone didn't sound friendly anymore. He wanted to have that easy conversation back with her. "So, before my stellar display of coordination, I was telling you about my time in the NFL."

"Were you? Oh, yes—the amazing quarterback drafted to the worst team in the league. How did that work out?"

"Terrible. I should have known better. I had the mistaken idea that maybe the team would turn around with the right players. Unfortunately, my team had no idea how to protect my quarterback position. I cringe just thinking about how many times I got sacked."

Nichole's pace slowed as he spoke. Barely glancing sideways, she said, "I'm sure it's hard to turn down the opportunity to become famous. I hope they paid you well for your trouble. How long did you play?"

"I didn't even make it through the first season. We'd won six games, but it cost us. Dearly. Several of our team had already been sidelined for injuries, and we were using several second-string players against a pretty formidable opponent. At the end of the third quarter, a right-side linebacker pierced the offensive line and hit me in the knees. It was a dirty move, and the refs didn't even flag him for it.

"I knew I was in trouble before I even hit the ground. I've never felt such pain as I did with that tackle. They carted me off the field, and I went straight to the hospital. I haven't played since."

"Ouch! What was the extent of your injury?"

He chuckled at the enthusiasm of her question. "I tore the anterior cruciate ligament and the meniscus. The only lucky break I got was that there happened to be a specialist visiting the hospital when I arrived. He took an immediate interest in my case and performed a ground-breaking surgery to fix it. I might have a few scars, but at least I don't have a permanent limp or much residual pain."

"Interesting! I wonder if I know the doctor. Who was he?"

"Dr. Stephen Barnes."

Nichole abruptly stopped and turned to face Markson. "Seriously?"

"Do you know him?" He tried to read her expression to discover if she were upset or excited.

"Know him? Absolutely! He's the one who performed my knee surgery. He told me he'd only ever done the procedure two times before mine, but both were a complete recovery."

"Wow! He told me I was the first. Good grief, I didn't care about it being experimental; I just wanted to get back on the field." Markson's mind raced straight back to when he laid in his hospital bed, watching his team get annihilated game after game. Their season ended with six and ten—dead last, again.

A bird calling out overhead snapped his thoughts back to the present. His eyes focused on Nichole's, and only then did he grasp what she'd said. "Wait! Why did you have to have knee surgery? Please don't tell me it kept you out of the Olympics."

CHAPTER 4
NICHOLE

Nichole's eyebrows twitched, her mood shifted as she recalled the most challenging time in her life. Hearing Mark's story had touched a raw nerve in her. All too well, she knew the pain he'd experienced. Although she hadn't believed she'd have a cross-country track career, she had set her sights on winning an Olympic gold medal. And with her track times, she'd had a decent chance of achieving her goal.

"I'm afraid so, but I didn't get as far as you did in my goal. It was my Junior year in college when it happened. I'd just finished a great practice session, and my teammates wanted to go out to dinner. I had a physics exam to study for, so I declined and went back to my dorm alone." She'd often wondered how her life would look had she chosen to join her teammates.

Sniffing, she refocused and returned to her story. "I'd already been out later than I planned, and I really wanted to get several hours of studying done before going to bed. I was in a hurry and raced up the stairs two at a time like I'd done hundreds of times before. But this time, I slipped on a piece of pepperoni someone dropped on the tread."

She paused, still embarrassed that she had to include that minor detail. It sounded so stupid, almost as bad as slipping on a banana peel. A glance at Mark made her think twice; he wasn't smiling because of it. His expression was concerned, tinged with anger. Did he believe that someone had deliberately left it there as she had innumerable times? Maybe.

She had to look away to continue; he was too distracting. "Anyway, like a fool, I wasn't using the handrail. I twisted as I fell, and the side of my knee cracked down on the edge of the stair. Instantly, I knew it wasn't good. I'm sure you can relate to the pain engulfing every nerve ending."

Nichole reached out to rub her knee, long healed, but just talking about it made it almost feel real again. "I can't tell you how long I sat there, crying and writhing in pain. I didn't have my cell phone, and my mind wasn't clear enough to call anyone anyway. Eventually, a girl came down the stairs and found me. She called the campus security, and they carted me off by ambulance to the hospital."

She didn't add that that was only the beginning of the worst part of that year. Mark didn't need to know every sordid detail. But, he could relate to her injury. It did feel good to speak to someone who understood, even though she wouldn't wish that injury on her worst enemy.

Markson shook his head and whistled softly. "What was the extent of your injury?"

Sighing, she answered, "The same thing as yours. When you told me, my mind went right back to that awful moment."

"Yeah. Isn't that weird how you can go for a long time without giving it a single thought, then boom, you're right there again. I've always called them 'gotcha' moments in my past—the ones you repeat in your mind in the smallest, most vivid details." Markson took several more steps, his shoes loudly crunching down the loose gravel, contemplating their shared experiences. "Were you in Miami then?"

"No, I was in Orlando. I didn't realize that Dr. Barnes moved around so much, but I guess it makes sense. He'd have to travel to wherever the people had the injury he was trying to fix. I still can't believe we had the same doctor at almost the same time. He said the other two surgeries in his case study were only six weeks before mine."

Nichole could hardly comprehend the astronomical chances of meeting Mark—in Atlanta, of all places. Their shared painful experience had pioneered a breakthrough surgical procedure. Not only that, the experience changed the course of her life and his as well.

The drawn-out silence became awkward. Mark's question almost startled her. "How has your knee been since you recovered? I haven't seen you limping."

She almost laughed. After all, she'd just run a half-marathon down a mountainside without any complaint.

"It's been perfect, but I wasn't able to run as I had before. I didn't fully recover until after I graduated. But by then, I'd decided to go to nursing school. After watching them in action, I knew I wanted to help people like that."

Nichole glanced over to see Mark's reaction. Seeing him nod, she added, "But my dad disapproved. He wanted me to come to work at his business. He'd been looking forward to the day I graduated so I could join the team. I dreaded telling him, and his reaction was exactly as I imagined it would be."

Her heart clenched tightly, just thinking back to that moment. It was the lowest point in her life to disappoint the only father she'd known. She owed him so much, and she'd repaid him with a broken promise. In a whisper, she added,

"I should have stuck with his plan. If I had, then maybe he wouldn't be fighting for his life in the hospital right now."

Markson scoffed. "You know that doesn't even make sense, right?"

Narrowing her eyes, she looked up at him. Who was he to make a judgment about her? "I'm sure it doesn't to you, but I should have been watching over things better. If I'd been working with him, then maybe he wouldn't have needed to bring on a partner. I could have saved him so much grief."

Mark's expression remained firm as he pressed his point. "Look, I'm sure your dad would be the first one to say that you should follow your dreams. Can you honestly say you would have been happier working at your dad's company?"

Nichole thought about Mark's comment, not that she hadn't asked herself the same thing countless times. Finally, she shook her head. "No, but I should have made more time for him."

Mark elbowed her playfully, the contact barely brushing her skin. "Again, he'd probably say differently."

She liked having physical contact with him. Sighing, she pushed Mark's bicep playfully. The hardness of his muscles surprised her into blurting what she intended to keep to herself. "You're really annoying. You know that?"

Markson's eyebrow playfully twitched. "I've heard that said about me before. I'll take it as a compliment."

"Well, it wasn't intended as one." Sighing, she added, "I still feel responsible for him losing his company. If I'd been there, I'm sure it wouldn't have happened."

"What's this? How did he lose his company?" His concern was quite evident in the way his voice rose.

Nichole couldn't understand Mark's sudden interest. After all, why would a corporate pilot care so much about the loss of a family company? It wasn't like he was personally responsible.

But they had plenty of time to kill, and maybe talking about it would alleviate some of her anger over the hostile takeover before she saw her dad. He didn't need the added stress of her righteous anger.

"Remember I said that Dad brought on a partner?" Seeing Mark nod, she continued, "Well, it turns out that guy was a con-artist. I never had a good feeling about him, but Dad said he was the salt of the earth kind of guy. Someone whose word was their bond. Yadda, yadda. Anyway, I never did like him. He gave me the creeps.

"Anyway, Sal had been working with Dad for about three years when everything started going haywire. At first, it was just little things like the inventory being wrong. Then, the bank accounts started showing discrepancies, as well. Sal kept saying they were clerical errors, and Dad believed him.

"About three months ago, Dad took a much-needed vacation and left Sal in charge. While he was away, Sal sold Dad's company and took off with all of the money. Nobody has seen him since.

"If I ever meet the man who stole my father's business, I swear I'll wring his neck with my bare hands. Who does that kind of thing, anyway? I'm sure he's some greedy scumbag just as unscrupulous as Sal.

"I told Dad that he should take the new owners to court, but Dad refused. He used his 'what's done, is done' saying and didn't do anything. His passivity makes me want to scream.

"Anyway, I was stuck in a job rotation until yesterday. I planned on flying home soon to be with him when he called this afternoon to tell me he was going to the hospital. And that brings us to where you came into the picture."

Nichole stopped walking to scan their surroundings. After following the creek downhill for quite some time, this seemed like the best place to cross. If they were both agile enough, they'd be able to skip across on the rocks and stay dry. She knew she could do it, but the question came as to whether or not Mark could.

"I sure hope you're still as light on your feet as you were in your football days." She set her hands on her hips and practically challenged Mark to agree.

"How come I get the feeling you're talking about crossing this river?" He looked away from her to investigate this new obstacle.

"Well, we can't keep following it, or we'll never make it to Gatlinburg. I estimated that we were about ten miles out—as the crow flies—when we went down. That means we'll have three ridges and a wide valley to cross before we make it there."

"Whoa, whoa! Who said anything about walking the whole way to Gatlinburg? I thought the idea was to get somewhere with cell coverage and then call for help. Or at the very least, we'd find someone's house and ask to use their landline."

Something inside Nichole snapped. Laughter bubbled out of her lips, and she chuckled so hard that tears filled her eyes. She bent over, hands resting on her knees as she struggled to remain standing.

Markson really was the city-slicker she had initially imagined. He'd obviously never lived anywhere where conveniences simply didn't exist. What could she expect? As handsome and kind as he was, he had to have some faults. Ignorance of country living wasn't the worst offense he could have, but it sure did strike her funny bone.

"I don't see what's so amusing."

His defensive response set her off again until she found herself sitting on the ground, continually wiping her eyes clear of the tears that overflowed. She had to get a grip on herself, but the release had been long overdue.

Coughing several times, she finally managed to compose herself enough to say, "If you hadn't noticed, there isn't anything out here, Mark. No people, no cell service. Nothing. The sooner you come to terms with that, the better off we'll be. We're just fortunate neither of us was hurt in the crash so that we can walk the ten miles."

"Well, when you put it that way—what are we waiting for? We're burning daylight. Lead the way, and I'll follow." He stretched out his hand and pulled her up to her feet. "And if you fall in, I'll rescue you."

"Hah! It's more likely that you'll fall in. Pay careful attention and try to keep up." With that, Nichole grinned and took the first leap onto the rock several feet from shore. As nimble as a mountain goat, she sprung from rock to rock, maintaining her momentum until she reached the other side. Gaining the solid ground, she barely managed to turn before Mark landed right beside her.

Nodding slowly, she said, "Very nicely done. We'll make a proper mountain man out of you yet."

Markson blew on his knuckles before scuffing them over his chest. "Piece of cake. Try to make the next one more challenging, would you?"

"Ugh, don't get cocky. It'll bite you in the butt. Hey, how's your hand doing?" She reached out toward his fist and waited for him to present it to her. After removing the almost dry moss, she nodded with pleasure that the blood had clotted nicely. "Does it still sting?"

"Nope. It's fine. Let's get walking. I don't relish the idea of spending the night out here."

"I couldn't agree more. However, it's a wonderful way to spend the night outside of the city's hustle and bustle. You should try it sometime."

Markson fell into step beside Nichole. "I'll have to take your word for it. So, what kind of business did your dad have?"

Hearing his voice almost falter on the question seemed odd, but then again, everything about this day had gone strangely.

The day's strains must be playing tricks on her, but it still hurt to think about how upset her dad had been when he'd heard about the outright theft of his company.

CHAPTER 5

MARKSON

The sickening roiling in his stomach made it hard for Markson to make his comment sound nonchalant. Even to his ears, his question sounded strained. Surely, this had to be a different company. Sal was a pretty common name, right? The incessant stinging in his palm faded into insignificance as he hoped she'd say something to prove him wrong.

"It's not his company anymore, but to humor you, he engineered and manufactured specialized equipment. It started with heavy-duty trailers, then moved to transportable feed bins, then log splitters, and he began moving into airplane tugs just when Sal came on board." Nichole sighed; her gaze grew distant.

With each word, Markson felt sicker and sicker. This had to be the acquisition his intern had identified and handled. How many other businesses in Gatlinburg would manufacture the same types of products? Time to rip off the bandage and ask the one thing he really didn't want to know.

Clearing his throat to get her attention back to the present, he asked, "What was his business called?"

Nichole seemed to deflate even further as she sighed again. "JDM Manufacturing. He was becoming one of the biggest employers in Gatlinburg, which is really sad because those people depend on their jobs. It's not like they have an abundance of employment choices out this far."

No denying the truth now. This is what he got for letting an intern and a division head spearhead a project. Typically, he would personally oversee all acquisitions, but he'd been inundated with projects, including the one he was initially flying out to inspect when Nichole diverted his flight to Gatlinburg. The luxury treehouses would have to wait since this new problem would clearly take precedence.

What kind of legal trouble was waiting on his doorstep now? He'd have to review the contracts to see what had transpired with the deal. Hopefully, the intern had kept sufficient notes to track his progress.

The right thing to do would be to return the company immediately. But what if Nichole didn't have the facts right?

How was he supposed to find out the truth if nobody knew what had happened with Sal?

Immediately, his mind turned to his good friend, Stephen. He had both the talent and the time to investigate a missing person's case. Once they got out of here, he'd get in touch with him. Until then, he needed more information.

In all of the years since he'd started his venture capitalist business, he'd never had anything like this happen. It might be time to retake complete control of his company. Luckily, he didn't have any personal relationship that would suffer from his newfound use of his time.

His sixty-hour workweeks would have to return to his previous eighty-hour status. Not that he minded. He loved the hunt and the risk. What he didn't want was to be involved in a scandal or a court case. Both of which seemed imminent if Nichole's story panned out.

But, he wouldn't mind spending more time with Nichole, if only to get more information about what happened. Maybe he'd even stick around to talk with her dad, assuming he was feeling okay. Besides, after spending so many hours with Nichole, he wanted to make sure her dad would be alright.

"How did your dad come up with the company name?" Markson didn't know why he was asking, maybe simply to keep her talking while trying to figure out his next move. He'd have to tell her who he really was, but he'd wait until the right moment. With her vivid description of how she felt about the person who bought the company, he didn't relish the idea of being left to fend for himself in the woods.

Already, he didn't like the darkness pressing in like a bad omen all around them. Nichole's steps remained firm and swift, forcing Markson to stumble after her. Maybe she could see in the dark, but he couldn't. He needed to stay in her good graces until they got out of this mess.

"My dad named it after himself. His name is Jacob Del Monroe. I wonder how long it'll take the new owners to rip down his name and change it to something else."

Her rhetorical question added another item to Markson's to-do list. He'd make sure to halt any actions where JDM Manufacturing was concerned until he could sort out the details. All of the employees would remain in place, continuing with their assignments until further notice.

They crested another steep incline just as the moon began to rise to their left. The thin strands of light seemed a welcome change to the gloomy forest interior. Markson almost sighed with relief at the additional light. Nichole turned to face the heavenly body, its light turning her skin into a fine, white marble, further enhancing her natural beauty.

Seeing the pain etched across her face reminded him of his predicament. He'd do just about anything to take that pain away from her. She'd already lost enough in her life. If he could undo the damage he'd inadvertently caused, then maybe she wouldn't want to commit a criminal act against him anymore.

He had to tell her the truth. Maybe the darkness would help him through this unusual problem. She'd already admitted that she didn't want him to get separated from her.

"We should keep moving. I think we're about halfway. If we keep up this pace, we can get there before midnight. We're lucky to have a full moon to help light the way." Nichole turned and smiled; her eyes crinkled with real emotion. Markson couldn't breathe, and he couldn't look away from her. He had to say something before he lost his nerve.

"Nichole, I think you need to know something about me," he started, wondering how he'd get through this without losing the tenuous friendship they'd forged.

"Oh, yeah? What's that? Don't tell me that you're actually a serial killer posing as a corporate pilot. Do you have duct tape in that emergency kit you're carrying?" Nichole laughed and shook her head. She turned and took one step away from the ridge—and dropped out of his sight with only a single, sharp squeal of fear and a sickening thud.

It happened so fast he didn't even have a chance to reach out a hand to try to catch her. "Nichole! Oh, please be okay! Nichole!" He heard her groan, both relieving and terrifying in equal measure.

"Don't move, Mark. I don't want you joining me on this ledge. I don't know if it'll hold both of us. Can you lie down, scoot forward, and reach over the ridge?"

Following her direction, he peered over the cliff to see Nichole had landed on a narrow rock outcropping. The moon's deceptive light had kept them from seeing the edge, making it only look like a dark patch of the slope. It didn't look like it went much deeper, maybe only another five feet, but it would still be difficult to extract her from the mountain's cleft.

Without thinking, he stretched his right hand down and felt Nichole's hand clasp onto it tightly. He ignored the fresh, lancing pain emanating from his palm; that was nothing compared to helping Nichole back to safety. With his other hand braced against the rock, he began pulling her up.

Thankfully, the universe decided to work with them for once. He brought her up far enough that she could leverage herself the rest of the way. He kept his hand on her arm until he was confident that she wouldn't falter and fall again. She remained seated as she scooted herself far enough away from the edge before Markson felt comfortable enough to remove his hand.

"Are you hurt, Nichole?" Kneeling, he hovered over her like a mother hen. He reached out toward her but paused when she started talking.

"I don't know yet. Give me a minute to get my bearings." Her voice trembled as she breathed deeply.

Only then did he notice how his fingers shook. For some reason, seeing Nichole disappear so suddenly was more frightening than the emergency landing in his jet. At least, with the airplane, he'd been in control, as tenuous as that control had been. Pilots trained for that type of emergency, but he didn't have any wilderness preparedness knowledge. He needed Nichole to be okay because he hated how helpless he felt.

Seeing her start to push herself off the ground, he jumped to his feet and offered his hand to assist. She took it and gingerly rose. He gritted his teeth against the instant pain in his hand. It only took Markson a second to realize they had a problem. From the way she favored her left side, he knew the fall had caused her a significant and debilitating injury.

"Tell me what hurts? How bad is it?" Markson hoped she wouldn't pretend like nothing was wrong; he could clearly see otherwise.

"I banged my knee on the way down. It might just be badly bruised, but I think I might have strained it." When she shifted toward the left, her knee buckled, and Markson's hand whipped out to cradle her elbow.

Great, now they were both injured, and they'd only been on the ground for a couple of hours. What else could happen to them before they reached safety? Markson breathed through a wave of concern and took charge of the situation.

"Whoa! Okay, let's take a breather and assess the damage before you manage to throw yourself off the cliff again. Do you want to sit down or stay standing? You're the medical professional here; just tell me what I need to do?" He couldn't just stand around and do nothing; that wasn't in his nature.

"Help me sit so I can roll up my pant leg."

Rather than watch her wince again, he swooped over and cradled her in his arms. She fit perfectly against his chest.

"Ouch, ouch!" she hissed at the sudden movement.

"I'm sorry, I thought this way might make things easier on you." He hardly even noticed her weight; she felt lighter than anything he used in his Crossfit workouts. He kneeled and gently set her on the ground.

"It might have been if you would have warned me first." Giggling, Nichole said, "I don't think that was quite necessary, but thank you anyway."

If she could joke, then maybe it wasn't as bad as he'd initially thought. "At your service. What's next?"

She quirked one eyebrow as she lifted her gaze to meet his. "Well, if you move out of what little light we have, I might be able to see my knee."

Dumbly looking over his shoulder, he spotted the moon and realized he cast a wide shadow across her prone body. Immediately, he scooted to his right and leaned forward to do his own inspection of her nicely shaped leg. "Please tell me that's not the knee you had the surgery on."

"No, it's not, but that might not be a blessing. I don't want to have trouble down the road with both of my knees. I'm sure you can understand." Her fingers lightly touched the offending area. They spider-crawled up her leg from mid-calf to mid-thigh and back down again, shifting clockwise for the return trip.

Yes, that would be true—one was bad enough. "Does your other knee bother you much? Mine's been nearly perfect. I only notice it when I'm in freezing weather. It's one reason I live in Atlanta." Markson clamped his mouth shut before he babbled any other nonsensical information.

Slowly, she straightened her leg; her face contorted in pain at full extension. Using her hands behind her knee, she lifted it to a fifteen-degree angle. Sighing loudly, she said, "I've got good news and bad news."

Inwardly groaning, Markson said, "Let's start with the good. I need some right about now."

An ironic smile lifted one side of her mouth. "Nothing is broken or torn."

Relief rushed through him. Maybe they could still make it to Gatlinburg sometime tonight, albeit much later if they'd have to travel slower for her. "That's really good. What's the bad news?"

"It's really a bad strain. Unless I can wrap it tightly, I'm afraid I won't be able to travel much more tonight. Do you have anything in your emergency kit? Any braces, wraps, or cloth of any kind?"

Markson immediately shrugged the pack off of his shoulders and turned until he sat beside her. The moonlight offered little help, but he already thought this was a lost cause. His fingertips touched the edges of the first-aid kit, and he pulled it out. "This is all I've got, but I think it only has gauze and sterile strips. Go ahead and check it out." He passed it to her and held his breath as she lifted the latch.

At this moment, he desperately hoped he was wrong, but he wasn't. After pulling out a pain-relief packet, she handed back the kit and sighed again. "Any other ideas?"

She tore open the foil wrap and popped the pills in her mouth, managing to swallow them dry.

Markson grimaced, imagining how awful that must have tasted. "Would you like some water? I've got some of that in here." He dropped the kit into the bag and fished out a bottled water.

"Better late than never. Thanks!" She grinned to take the sting of criticism away. Effortlessly, she twisted the cap off and took a long swig, swallowing several times before filling her mouth again and swooshing it around.

"Well, we could wrap a shirt around it. I'd choose yours, but that would be selfish. So, since I'm a gentleman, I'll gladly give you mine." In the distance, wolves began howling, piercing the silence of the night.

CHAPTER 6
NICHOLE

Nichole stared at him for a second before she burst out laughing, water spewing from her lips, having it land on herself and Mark in equal portions. Even though the movement painfully jarred her knee, she couldn't stop. Mark never ceased to amaze her with the outrageous things he said. She managed to say, "Gentleman! You're such a typical guy! It sounds like your buddies are calling for you."

"Seriously? You heard my phone?" Mark's face brightened with eagerness. He began patting his pants to locate the phone, shifting sideways to access it better.

"No, silly! I meant the wolves howling." His hopeful reaction made her feel bad for her lame joke, especially seeing his crestfallen look. She brushed ineffectually at the water across her thigh just for something to occupy her hand. She wanted to reach out to Mark, to apologize, but that wasn't her place.

Her gaze broke away from him to look toward the distant sound. The hunting call reminded her of the man at the crash. She was sure he wasn't still pursuing them, but he wasn't the only danger in the forest. "But, we should check for cell reception. We could use a miracle right about now."

The wind shifted and blew straight at them as if reminding her of their exposed position on the mountainside. They'd have to move to a more sheltered place if nothing else. Hopefully, she'd only have to rest for a few minutes, and they could resume their journey. Maybe the pain pills would provide her some measure of relief.

Inwardly, she cursed fate for delaying their trip yet again. Why would her luck turn so rotten at the very moment she wanted it to be perfect? Her dad needed her. Was she going to miss being there for him again?

Beside her, Markson growled in frustration. It wasn't lost on her that he sounded exactly like the wolves she'd compared him to earlier, but she didn't mention it. "Still nothing, huh?"

"Worse. My phone's dead. I don't understand it. I still had half a battery left when I last checked. Unbelievable!"

He looked like he was ready to throw his phone, and Nichole couldn't restrain herself. Reaching over, she grabbed his arm and pulled it down. "I think you were right." Just as she intended, his gaze turned to her; his expression puzzled as he tried to figure out what she was talking about.

"What?"

Valiantly resisting the urge to smile, she said, "I'm going to need your shirt if we're going to get any farther tonight." She didn't expect his immediate compliance, nor did she plan to become transfixed with staring at his perfectly muscled torso. Six-packs like his were only airbrushed onto magazine models—they didn't exist in real life. Maybe the moonlight was creating another illusion, but somehow she doubted it.

"Aren't you going to take it? I don't want to freeze for nothing." He shook the shirt to catch her attention.

With extreme effort, she dragged her eyes away from his chest and looked at the shirt. "You're right. I can't have you freezing out here. Forget I said anything. Put it back on."

"No way. I was only teasing. I promise I'm not the least bit cold. I'll even let you touch me if that's what it'll take to convince you. Give me your hand." He made to seize her hand, but she grabbed the shirt and moved away as fast as she could.

"I'll take your word for it." She busied herself with folding the soft, luxurious fabric and wrapping it tightly around her throbbing knee. It wasn't a perfect fix, but she did think she could bear her weight without too much trouble as long as they didn't have too far to go.

Her accidental touching of his chest at the river was enough to convince her she shouldn't tempt herself again. She'd felt something flare inside her at that encounter, but she didn't have the nerve to see where it would go. Besides, Mark would plan a flight back to Atlanta, and she'd probably never see him again.

She'd already experienced enough disappointment in the relationship department. The last thing she wanted was to start having feelings for someone who lived in another state. Everybody knew that long-distance relationships were a recipe for disaster. She had enough sense to steer clear of that scenario.

Wow, she'd really let her mind wander much farther than she planned. Her single status worked perfectly with her lifestyle and career. And she had pressing family matters that would occupy every waking moment of her time. She wasn't in any position to even think about getting involved with someone—even if he could be a candidate for the sexiest man of the year.

There, she'd admitted that he was handsome, sexy, and well-built while also protecting herself from any involvement.

She never said anything about being blind or delusional; she was a woman who could appreciate his physique and enjoy his company without expecting anything more. She expected the same thing from him, and so far, he hadn't disappointed her.

It might have been wishful thinking, but she began to believe the pain killers had started to kick in. Tentatively, she stretched out her leg, hands hovering beside her knee to support it if needed. It felt stiff, but she could live with that. Walking could be beneficial for keeping it loose, but only if she hadn't done any real damage.

If she'd had a choice, she would have waited, but the night was only getting darker, colder, and windier. They had miles to go, and no progress would happen as long as she remained lounging indolently on the ground. Rather than risk unnecessary injury, she held up her hand and asked, "Can you help me up? I want to test my weight to see if we can keep moving."

Nichole braced herself for the contact, all the while wondering if he felt the same connection between them when they touched. His skin practically buzzed with electricity. She'd heard about male magnetism, but she never thought it meant literal tingling.

He struck out his palm, the bright white light illuminating his flesh and showing her the wound now oozing fresh blood. "Good grief! You're bleeding again. Sit here and let me dress it properly with the first aid kit. If I would've known we had it before, I would have used that instead of the moss." How in the world had he been using his hand to help her without any complaint? She was altogether off her game to miss such an important detail as this.

Once again, Mark sat facing her, their knees brushing lightly. She shivered with the contact. Apparently, they didn't need bare flesh touching to get the same electric sensation. He pulled the bag closer and retrieved the medical kit.

Working on his hand helped her keep her eyes from wandering over to his bare torso. It really was unfair for him to be so perfectly sculpted. The moonlight cast shadows that only emphasized the rippling muscles. He wasn't even flexing, and the definition was still evident.

Did he work out much, or was he one of those guys who had a naturally well-muscled body? With his perfect physique, handsome face, and pleasant personality, she wondered where he hid his flaws. Nobody could have so many blessings without some significant hang-ups. At least in her experience, she'd never encountered anyone whose life mirrored Prince Charming.

In her element, she only needed a few minutes to get him properly bandaged. From the angry redness on the edges of the wound, it looked like it still had bacteria embedded in the cut. She hoped he didn't have an allergic reaction to the plant he'd grabbed. "I liberally applied the antiseptic ointment, but I'd suggest flushing it with hydrogen peroxide when we get into Gatlinburg. Are you ready to get going again?"

"You bet. Do you think you'll be okay? I don't mind carrying you. You're light as a feather."

The idea of being crushed next to his perfect chest had its appeal; she didn't trust herself to be so close to him. He didn't need to know that a well-sculpted chest was her kryptonite. Rather than admit her weakness, she laughed, forcing herself to sound amused. "Ha! Hardly. No, thanks. Although, it might be wise if you stay nearby just in case I stumble."

"Noted. I'll stick to you like glue. Besides, you're the only one who knows which direction to go, so there's that."

Nichole laughed with genuine humor while appreciating his gracefulness as he stood. She could easily imagine him playing football and wished she'd known him when he played. Taking his offered left hand, she rose, although not nearly as effortlessly as he had.

"How is it?" Mark's hand hadn't left her arm and his intent gaze at her leg made her feel even more self-conscious.

Slowly, she leveraged her weight equally onto both legs. Her left knee seemed sound, but standing still wouldn't put the same strain on it as walking down and up the hills they had yet to cross. "So far, so good."

Once again, she looked out across the wilderness below them. Pointing, she said, "Do you see those lights in the distance?" Hearing his hum of agreement, she added, "That's Gatlinburg. See? We don't have that far to go."

"Hmph. It still seems pretty far away to me. I'll take your word for it. Lead the way, and I'll be right at your side." She watched him zip up the bag and sling the handles over his shoulders once again.

Heat rose inside her as she watched the ripple of muscles at his movements. He had to know that his physique was distracting, yet he didn't seem to use it to his advantage. She startled when Mark asked, "Ready?"

"What? Oh! Yes. Let's go." She didn't foolishly step without looking this time. Surveying the ground carefully not to be deceived by the moon's false shadows, she picked the smoothest path leading down.

The loose shale rock made footing tricky. More than once, both of them slid for several feet without knowing how they would stop. Luckily, the land would rise enough to stop their uncontrolled descent. Unfortunately, this uncertainty made Nichole tense up, which only exacerbated her knee's trauma.

By the time they made it down to the meadow, Nichole almost cried out in relief. Every step sent lancing pains up the sides of her knee, every pause left her leg trembling, and she could no longer hide her limp. Mark's arm slid around her back and hugged her body close to his. Even with his assistance in taking most of her weight, the pain made her want to cry.

At any other time, the proximity of his bare chest crushed against her would have distracted her. Even inhaling his musky scent could not keep her sidetracked. Her knee forcibly reminded her of their dire situation.

She drew to a stop and sighed. How could her body have betrayed her? Yet, she only had herself to blame for foolishly walking off the side of the mountain. She knew better. Heck, first-year Girl Scouts knew better than to step without looking. But the damage was done, and so were her chances of seeing her dad that night. "I'm sorry, Mark. We're going to have to stop for the night. I can't go any farther."

"The offer still stands for me to carry you." Mark released her so he could move to face her. "I promise I don't mind. How much farther do we have to go?"

She shook her head, wishing she could accept his generous offer. "Miles. It's no use, Mark. We'll have to make camp and hope that resting my knee will allow us to resume our travels in the morning."

Mark looked away, glancing over his shoulder in the direction they were heading. She could see his indecision, maybe even a little apprehension.

Lifting her hand, she rested her palm against his tricep. She probably should have kept her hands to herself, but she hoped the unexpected physical contact would jar him out of whatever fear he experienced. "Remember how I said camping out here was something everyone should experience? Tonight's your night.

"Can you carry me across the meadow? We can make camp near the far treeline. I'll even show you how to start a fire. Too bad we don't have any marshmallows to toast. You don't happen to have any in your magic emergency kit, do you?"

CHAPTER 7
MARKSON

Summer camp when he was twelve was the last time Markson had roughed it in the wilderness overnight. But then, he'd had a log cabin, comfy bed, and a five-star Michelin chef making three meals a day for him—nothing to compare to this experience. And nothing at all like the luxury treehouse he'd planned on staying in in the Catskills.

"Sorry to disappoint. I'm plum out of marshmallows." The idea of doing something so mundane as toasting marshmallows would have made this unexpected outdoor sleepover much less intimidating.

"Well, I hope you have matches in your bag; otherwise, we'll have to resort to rubbing two sticks together."

Markson's eyes flicked back to Nichole's. He knew what she was trying to do. He responded in kind. "Yeah, it would make me feel terrible to watch you struggle with the sticks. It's a pretty warm night; maybe we don't even need a fire."

"Ha, ha. You might be warm now, but the temperature hasn't finished dropping, and you've been exerting yourself. A few hours of inactivity might change your mind. Besides, the fire's not so much for the heat as for protection from predators, both big and small."

Suitably chastised, Markson took matters into his own hands—literally. He bent over but paused before touching her. "Are you ready this time?" Seeing her nod, with extreme care, he picked her up. Once again, he crushed her against his chest, hardly noticing any difference in his stride with her slight weight and slim body.

The hours they'd spent together helped him feel more comfortable, especially knowing he could tease her. "Well, I guess it's too late for you. If a predator comes, I'm pretty big, and you're pretty small and incapacitated. Point me in the right direction so we can get settled."

Feeling Nichole's giggle lightened his mood. He hoped he'd helped her, too. But their night was far from over.

By the time he'd put Nichole down, scraped a large area clear of flammable debris using a piece of shale, and gathered enough kindling and firewood to Nichole's exacting specifications, he hardly looked forward to having the fire's heat. Sweat glistened from his body, running annoyingly into his eyes and down his back.

Dumping the last of the wood onto the medium-sized pile, he wearily dropped onto the ground. Only then did he notice Nichole had dug into the soft ground about eight inches and had started tenting the kindling in the center.

"Do you have matches?" She looked up through her long lashes. The moon's light made her impossibly beautiful, so much so that Markson took several seconds before he realized what she'd asked.

Feeling foolish for his delayed reaction, he stretched out his hand to pull the emergency bag closer. Although he'd assembled the contents of the bag himself, it had been almost a year since he'd gone through it. For the life of him, he couldn't recall if matches had been part of the ensemble.

With the bag unzipped, he began rifling through the contents. When that didn't produce the much-needed matches, he began hauling the items out as he came to them. "Ah, here's something we'll need." He held up his prize in the darkness.

"That looks too big to be matches and too small to be marshmallows."

"Right, but at least we'll have a hot meal. I'm assuming you're hungry." As if on cue, his stomach growled loud enough to compete with the chorus of crickets.

She brightened and leaned forward to investigate his treasure. "Starving. What is it?"

"I hope you're not a vegetarian because all I've got are two chicken and rice MRE's." He held them out for her to see better.

"That sounds amazing. I haven't had one of those in years. Unless you find those matches, we'll be eating them cold, though."

"Nope, I got the heater packs to go with them. All we need is an ounce of water, which we have in the bag. In a couple of minutes, we'll be filling our bellies with hot food."

Nichole's hands continued rubbing her knee as if testing for the extent of the injury. "That's good. With how much your tummy's been growling, I was going to suggest we start hunting for crickets. They're full of protein, you know."

Markson immediately looked at her, the search for the matches wholly forgotten. "You're not serious, are you?"

"Absolutely. Of course, you'd have to find a carcass and dig them out of it, but we'd have food."

She had to be pulling his leg. Nothing would ever convince him to eat crickets, no matter how much his stomach protested. Besides, he'd probably throw them up anyway.

Giggles punctuated the still night air. Markson sighed with relief and continued his search. "Whew, you really had me going there for a second. I mean, I know they eat crickets in foreign countries, but I'd rather go hungry."

The matches continued to elude him, which only aggravated him further. He probably should have started getting their MREs ready since hunger made him more ill-tempered than usual. Irritated beyond reason, he finally turned the bag to dump the contents on the ground.

One by one, he inspected each item. Paracord, hatchet, hammer, knife, small handsaw, water filter straw, tool kit, tarp, glow sticks, scissors, flares, multi-tool, medical handbook, and first aid kit all went back into the bag. Two water bottles, a thermal blanket, a flashlight, and the flint striker stayed out beside him.

He brandished the flint striker and said, "This is one step above rubbing sticks together." Hoping for better luck, he grabbed the flashlight and flicked the switch. The orange beam of light lasted all of two seconds before it flickered and died. "So much for that; I guess I should've changed those batteries out." He dropped the useless tube back into the bag, disgusted with himself for allowing this oversight.

"What's this?" Nichole reached over and plucked a small, neon-yellow tube from the ground that had rolled next to Markson's leg. She held it up for both of them to see.

"That's it. Those are the waterproof matches. Thank goodness. Good job, Nichole. You just saved me the embarrassment of trying to use that dumb flint striker. I've only ever watched a video on how to use it. And that guy had a wad of dryer lint to light." There he was, babbling again. This behavior had to stop before she thought he was a complete moron.

Raising one eyebrow, she pointedly looked at him. "You do realize you're ruining my previous opinion of making a mountain man out of you. But hey, while you have the first aid kit handy, get me a gauze pad and an alcohol wipe."

"Did you hurt yourself again?" Markson quickly complied while wondering what she'd done to herself while just sitting there.

Nichole took the items. With a practiced motion, she unwrapped the gauze and stuck it under the tripod of sticks. She then pulled out a match to have it ready to use. Finally, she opened the alcohol wipe, stuck it under the gauze, and lit the match as fast as she could.

The alcohol lit instantly but quickly burned off, but not before the gauze caught fire. The tendrils of fire wicked up the kindling. Nichole leaned over and gently blew on the fire, coaxing the flames higher.

Markson watched, mesmerized by her efficiency and skill. She must have done that hundreds of times to make it look so effortless. "I'm glad one of us has some survival skills."

She grinned, still leaning forward over the fire. Looking up at him, she said, "Yeah, I watched a video on it."

Markson almost called her out on the admission until he spotted the glint of humor in her eyes. Rather than embarrass himself further, he waved the two MRE boxes. "At least I brought the food." He broke the seals on the box tops and began getting the meals ready.

It bothered him more than he liked to admit that Nichole's strengths seemed to emphasize his weaknesses. He hated being at a disadvantage, but at least Nichole didn't throw it back in his face like so many other girls would have. Plus, he admired her quiet competence.

Within five minutes, they were eating next to the fire, which had grown hot enough that they'd had to move farther away from it. The front of Markson's torso grew hot, but the exposed skin on his back had grown chilled. To make matters worse, the biting flies and mosquitos were making a feast off of him faster than he could eat his MRE.

After swatting his shoulder again, Markson said, "I thought that smoke was supposed to repel these little beasts. I'm getting eaten alive."

"I'm so sorry. Let me give you back your shirt. Since we're spending the night here, I'm sure my knee won't need the extra support." Nichole looked around for someplace to put her pouch of food.

Markson immediately regretted saying anything. He knew his shirt added compression to her knee. "No way. You keep that on. I'll use the thermal blanket."

Putting action to his words, he unwrapped the package and unfurled it to drape the flimsy silver foil over himself. It crackled every time he moved, but at least the insects decided to leave him alone long enough for him to finish his meal in peace. They fed the empty food containers to the fire.

While this outing didn't compare in the slightest with his childhood camping experience, he found himself flinching at every twig snapping and every owl hooting. Nichole appeared as composed as ever, so he forced himself to relax and take his cues from her.

Nichole pointed out across the valley. "Have you ever seen anything like that in Atlanta?"

Following the direction of her outstretched arm, he looked over the fire and out into the distance. Small lights flickered all over the place in a strange synchronized dance. "Are those fireflies?"

"Yep. Have you seen them before?"

Markson watched, mesmerized, for several seconds before replying. His voice reflected his awe. "Not like this. It's almost like the redneck version of the Northern Lights."

Nichole chuckled. "I've never heard it put quite that way. I'm going to have to tell my dad—" She clamped her lips shut, and her expression immediately sobered.

"Hey, we've been over this before. Don't borrow trouble. Okay?" Markson couldn't stop himself from scooting until he sat right next to her. The plastic annoyingly crackled as he put his arm over her shoulders and hugged her close to his side.

"It's so hard not knowing what's going on. He's the only family I have left."

"I know you're scared. Is your husband with him?"

Nichole tried to pull away, but Markson held her firmly against his side. "What are you talking about? I don't have a husband."

"Oh, well, your boyfriend then."

He felt her head shake and her body tense. "I don't have one of those either. It's just my dad and me."

He felt his heart lighten at her admission. "Hmm. Well, you've got me. I'm here right now. I'll stay with you until you tell me to leave." How could he convince her that he meant every word he said?

"You're not obligated to do that. I know you've got a life of your own. You don't need me hijacking your time. Hey, your hand is scorching. How bad is that cut hurting? It might be getting an infection." She twisted to reach for him, but he moved it out of her grasp.

"Don't worry about me. Why don't you tell me what those fireflies are doing?"

"I know what you're trying to do." She sighed, and her body relaxed against his side. "Fine. Adult fireflies only live for about two weeks. This is their mating dance before they lay their eggs and die. It's both beautiful and tragic knowing that their whole life comes down to this last display."

Well, that conversation didn't end the way he'd hoped. He wanted to keep her thoughts away from dying, and he'd forced her to talk about it. Smooth, really smooth. Wracking his mind for a safer subject, he asked, "Why don't you tell me about your last boyfriend?"

Immediately, he wished he could take it back. Why would he blurt out something so insensitive? If her experience were anything like his own, it held enough hurt and disappointment to fill an Olympic-sized swimming pool.

Her shoulders minutely stiffened before she seemed to wilt in on herself. She leaned forward with her chin resting on her hand and her elbow on her knee. "You mean my one and only boyfriend?"

Markson's hand slipped down to the indent of her slim waist, and he chuckled at her joke. "I don't believe that for a second."

She tilted her head until she looked directly at him. The fire merrily crackling and casting a soft light across her saddened expression. "I know. Sad, but true. Jaxson was my only long-term boyfriend."

"I've got to hear this story. Do tell." Markson settled in, prepared to hear why this stunning woman only had a single boyfriend. Maybe he would glean her tragic flaw with the story. Otherwise, he couldn't see any reason why this attractive, smart, career-oriented woman didn't have a string of men vying for her notice.

CHAPTER 8
NICHOLE

"We met in college during my Sophomore year. I thought we were the perfect match since we were both on the track team. But I soon found out that Jaxson didn't share the same passion for the sport as I did. He liked running, but he enjoyed partying even more."

Nichole weighed her words. How much did she want to reveal about her failed relationship? Her father had always pressed her for details about why they broke up, but it hurt too much then. Over the years since, she'd managed to forget the most painful parts and only recalled them now when asked point-blank.

Sighing, she decided to think of this as an impromptu therapy session. Having nature surrounding her and a stranger to hear her tales of woe seemed like the perfect combination to restore her soul to health again. Still, she couldn't convince herself to look at Mark as she talked; that made it feel too personal.

Closing her eyes, she let the fire's heat soak into her. "Jaxson was the most popular guy on the team. Everybody liked him. Like bees to a flower on a hot summer day, I admit I gravitated to him just like everyone else. But I wasn't planning on getting involved with him.

"I turned him down several times before he finally convinced me to go out to dinner and a movie with him. It was just after midterms, and I didn't have much studying to do. I gave in and discovered I really enjoyed spending time with him.

"He was funny and attentive. He opened doors for me and made me feel special. He even planned every date. We'd been going out for a couple of months when he asked if I wanted to go to Disneyworld with him. Who wouldn't want to go to the happiest place on earth, right?" Nichole scoffed, hesitating several seconds before continuing.

"All the while I'd been going to college, not once had I been to any of the theme parks. Ever since I was little, I'd wanted to see the Epcot center. I suggested it to Jaxson, and he practically ridiculed me for suggesting it. He said, 'That's for old people. I want to go on the rides. I really want to show you the newest attractions. I think you'll love it.'"

Rolling her head to the side, she opened her eyes and looked at Mark for the first time since beginning her story. "That should have been my first clue that he and I weren't compatible. But I was naïve."

She grabbed the bottled water, twisted off the top, and took a gulp. Sucking the excess moisture from her upper lip, she put the bottle down again. "After we went to everything he wanted to see at Disney, we still had one afternoon left. Once again, I suggested going to Epcot. Jaxson threw a fit and finally said, 'Jeez, you're like a broken record. Let's just go already so you'll shut up about it.'"

"I didn't tell him how much his words hurt me. Besides, I thought once we got there, he'd discover that he liked it. Boy, was I wrong. From the moment we entered the hydroponics ride, he wouldn't stop poking fun at everything the tour guide said. I was ashamed even to be sitting next to him with the way people kept looking at us. It was a mortifying experience. By the time we got out of there, I was furious. I'd never seen him act so juvenile, and I let him have it.

"Once I finished, he got right in my face, stinky breath and all, and told me that I should be grateful for his attention at all. Any girl would take my place in a heartbeat. He stalked off and left me standing there gaping after him.

"I found a bench in the shade to wait for him to return. I was too furious to cry, but his words stuck with me, squeezing my heart harder and harder. It wasn't until the park was getting ready to close that I realized he wasn't coming back. He'd left me there to find a way home by myself.

"Obviously, I couldn't call my dad since he was in Gatlinburg. And, I didn't want to admit to my friends what Jaxson had done, so I didn't call them either. Finally, I ended up calling a car service and spent almost a hundred dollars that I didn't have to spare just to get back to my dorm.

"That poor driver must have thought I was a lunatic. I cried almost the entire way. He turned up the music, probably to drown out the sounds of my sobbing. Once I paid him, he sped away from the campus without a single word to me."

Her heart hammered against her ribs just thinking about that awful day. But she knew how it all ended, and it wasn't going to get easier to tell. "The next day, Jaxson came running up to me, acting all concerned. He fawned all over me, apologizing for walking away and for being a general idiot. Then he asked me why I left him. He said he searched and searched the park for me and finally convinced himself that

I left without him. Of course, it was all a lie. I hadn't moved from where he'd left me until I didn't have a choice. Later, I discovered that he went straight back to the campus and slept with another girl on the track team. But I didn't know anything about that until way later."

Mark inhaled sharply through his nostrils. "What a scumbag. Tell me where he lives so I can break his legs for you." He sprung from the ground, stomping his way back and forth beyond the fire from her. His righteous anger would have been more effective had the plastic thermal blanket not been flying out behind him like some deranged superhero's cape.

Nichole's eyes followed his progress, a small smile tugging at the corners of her mouth. It was nice having someone angry at Jaxson's terrible behavior. None of her college friends had stood by her side. Of course, Jaxson poisoned all of them against her before she said a single word. People tended to believe whatever he said, never once questioning the truth of the matter. At the time, it had frustrated and angered her, but now, she couldn't care less.

"Thanks for the offer, but I wouldn't worry about him. The last I heard, he was bagging groceries at the local convenience store. Sit down; you're making me tired." She patted the dirt beside her, hoping he'd return to the spot he'd vacated.

Shifting even a little bit jarred her bandaged knee, shooting sharp pains up and down her leg. Worry for herself compounded with the fear for her father weighed heavily on her shoulders. How was she supposed to take care of him if she couldn't even walk? And, more importantly, how were they ever going to get help if she couldn't move from this spot?

Markson skirted the fire and dropped gracefully back to his former spot. His proximity immediately refocused the direction of her thoughts. This time, he held out the thermal blanket and said, "Do you want to share this? It does a great job deterring the biting insects."

She rather liked the idea of sharing—he'd be that much closer to her—another random thought to shock her usually stoic senses.

Having him close felt good. She'd forgotten how nice it was to have a friend to confide in. Not that Mark was her friend, but she'd like to think they might become friends.

Maybe even something more. Where had that come from? Did she want to see where things could go with Mark? Her heart pounded harder just considering the question. Besides, she'd already ruled him out based on where he lived. Right?

"That sounds good. Thanks." How much more did Mark want to hear about her disastrous relationship? Surely, he'd heard more than enough.

But Mark's next question disabused her of that notion. "Please tell me you dumped that loser right then and there."

With a chuckle devoid of any amusement, Nichole shook her head. "Sadly, no. I forgave him, and we continued to date for almost another year. We didn't go back to Disney together, but he did take a group of friends there and didn't invite me. He said it was because he knew I had to study for a biochem exam, but it hurt all the same.

"He did stuff like that pretty often. He'd use my studying as an excuse to make plans without me. I was getting pretty sick of it, but it would sound petty of me to insist he stick around waiting for me to be ready. I'm not a clingy girlfriend. I'd seen enough of that around campus to know I'd never behave so foolishly with someone I cared about.

"So, Jaxson did whatever he pleased, and I focused on running and studying. This cycle went on month after month until summer vacation rolled around. I'd made plans to go home for a few months, but Jaxson had other ideas. We argued over it, but we weren't getting anywhere with it, and I finally left.

"I thought maybe we'd broken up since I didn't hear a single word from him for the entire three months we were apart. At first, I'd cried because he didn't call, and then I cried because I was happy that he didn't. I was a mess of mixed-up emotions. By the time I returned to the dorms to begin my Junior year, I'd resigned myself to being single again."

"Good riddance," Markson piped in. His hand reached over and squeezed the back of Nichole's hand where it rested against her thigh. She didn't mind; it felt nice to have his physical support. She turned her hand over, intertwined her fingers in his, and gave his hand a gentle, friendly squeeze.

"Unfortunately, we weren't over. Jaxson appeared at my dorm with smiles and flowers."

Markson groaned, and his hand squeezed hers. Nichole darted a glance over at him, her lips curling up in a rueful smile. His eyes spoke of the pain he felt for her. She had to finish this chapter. She had to tell him the worst part.

"He told me how much he missed me and couldn't wait to hear about my vacation in Gatlinburg. He made it seem like I left, and he was sitting around pining for me. And I was dumb enough to be guilted into believing him.

"Just like before, he made plans without me, using my studies as his excuse. We spent the most amount of time together when we were running and training for track. But then I got injured and didn't return to track. He never once came to see me at the hospital. He actually broke up with me with a text message just as I was getting prepped for surgery. I guess it was a good thing I was doped up with the anti-anxiety drugs, or I might have fallen apart.

"I never realized how much power his words had on me. When people would repeat what he said as true, I had no defense against it because I couldn't understand it. I didn't want to fight. I wanted to let it all go. My heart was tired from all of it. I needed to stop all of the chatter and felt like I'd served my sentence. I wanted someone who would protect me, not someone who would release dogs on me."

Nichole stared at the flames flickering from the burning wood. Occasionally, little sparks would rise and float away, almost looking like the fireflies still dancing in the distance. She imagined each one of those sparks was an unfulfilled dream from her life. At first, they were bright and full of hope, only to wither and die without anyone noticing.

How had she let all of her dreams slip away? Was she broken inside? Jaxson sure led her to believe she would be nothing without him. But she'd put that behind her. She had a career—something he couldn't claim for himself.

Recalling so many long-forgotten details about Jaxson didn't cause painful constrictions in her heart anymore. At least now, surrounded by her beautiful, expansive wilderness, she could let the wind take her problems away where nobody would ever find them. Inhaling deeply, the smoke-scented air brought her back to her happiest days. If only she could recapture her youth, where her dreams for a happily-ever-after still seemed possible.

Maybe coming back home was exactly what she needed to reboot her life. While her knee healed, she and her dad could plan their next move. If he didn't want to fight for the company he'd built from the ground up, then maybe they could work on building something together.

As much as she loved being a nurse, she loved her father more. Thinking about his current health scare forced her to admit that he wouldn't be around forever. She'd do anything to spend the rest of his life by his side.

The logs shifted in the fire, causing an eruption of sparks to fly free. As if this was the release she'd been seeking, Nichole's thoughts returned to the present. She'd been so engrossed she'd completely forgotten about Mark. With a shiver, she turned her head to discover Mark's face only inches from her own.

Her gaze dropped to his mouth, her bottom lip automatically drawing up between her teeth as she inhaled sharply. What would those perfect lips feel like on her own? Would that stubble tickle against her chin?

Most likely, she'd never find out. "So, tell me about your wife," Nichole said.

CHAPTER 9

MARKSON

Her question came so unexpectedly, Markson threw his head back and laughed. Leave it to her to ruin the mood he'd hoped to create. But really; what chance did he think he had with her? What right did he have to take advantage of her vulnerable moment? That kind of behavior followed closely on the heels of Jaxson's.

But, the way she'd looked at him gave him hope before her question slapped him back to reality. Maybe her feelings for him had changed. He'd take any improvement on that front. The more Nichole shared with him, the harder his instinct to protect her kicked in.

Not that he believed she needed any protection. He didn't know of any women as strong or as brave as she was. But she'd looked so vulnerable while she stared silently at the flames. He'd never seen anyone quite so beautiful, both inside and out.

Even without his conscious decision, he knew he wanted to be with her. Yet, this idea was so foreign; it made him want to run as far away as possible. Luckily, the expansive, lonely wilderness surrounding them kept him firmly seated next to her.

Plus, there was the little problem with his true identity. He hadn't meant to give Nichole the impression of only being a pilot; she'd come up with that all on her own. More than anything, he wanted to tell Nichole the truth about his company and his life. But if he did, he ran the real risk of her attempting to strangle him in his sleep. Hopefully, if she got to know him better, then she'd listen to his side of the story before trying to inflict any bodily harm.

Besides, sleep seemed like an unlikely prospect for him, given the various animal noises nearby and echoing through the surrounding mountains. Even though Nichole seemed at ease, he kept wondering how many predators lurked just out of the firelight's range. Were they biding their time, waiting for them to relax before making their move? Isn't that what happened in the movies? There had to be some element of truth, or people wouldn't fall for it.

"So, I guess from your lack of answer, you *are* married." Nichole shifted, putting several inches of space between them. If their shared blanket had been wider, he felt confident she would have gone farther.

Markson shook his head, fighting another urge to laugh. "Sorry to disappoint you. I'm very much single. I don't even have an ex-wife. In fact, my dating life is every bit as sad as yours, I'm afraid.

"Come closer. You're letting in the cold air." He gestured to convince her to return. "If it'll make you feel any better, I'll tell you about my last girlfriend. Okay, maybe the one before that, because I think you'll find that one more interesting."

Nichole cocked her head to the side as if considering his proposal. After only a second, she slid back into her former spot, but she kept her face turned toward the fire. "I'm listening. Although, you've already admitted to having at least twice as many relationships as I've had."

Markson grinned at her observation, knowing she wasn't looking. He cleared his throat, trying to restrain another chuckle. He was afraid that if he didn't contain himself, Nichole might move away again, and he rather enjoyed having her resting against his side like they really belonged together. Of course, he was the only one imagining their future, but he'd accept that until she came around.

"I met Jill at the gym. She and I were on the same Crossfit training circuit, so it would have been impolite for me to ignore her. It was her first time at the gym, and she asked me to help her.

"I thought she meant it was her first time at *that* gym, but what she left out was that she only came there to bump into me. After we broke up, I discovered that she'd been stalking me, trying to create an opportunity for us to meet. It turned out she absolutely hated Crossfit and any form of exercise.

"Anyway, I asked her to lunch, and she seemed like a nice enough girl. One thing led to another, and we started dating, but it wasn't long before I noticed some alarming traits. She only wanted to go places where there were lots of people to see us. Jill was very clingy, like a second skin.

"When people looked at us, she would preen and giggle, but she was like a different person—almost a Jeckle and Hyde syndrome when we were alone. When it was just the two of us, she spent most of her time on her phone, almost ignoring me.

"At first, I didn't know what to make of this, but I tried my best to overlook it. But sometimes, she would do things that I couldn't ignore. Jill would shamelessly flirt with other men while I was standing right there. But, goodness help me, if I even stood in the same room with another attractive girl, she would come unglued.

"Again, I didn't do anything to correct her behavior. I wasn't her father, and it wasn't my place. It's not like we were married."

Markson paused to glance at Nichole. He'd purposely used that phrase to see how she reacted. As he hoped, she smirked.

"Oddly enough, I also took her to Epcot. When you told me about your experience with Jaxson, it felt like you were telling my story. She reacted almost as poorly as he did the whole time we were there. I thought the entire hydroponics exhibit was fascinating, but I wanted to divorce myself from her company during the tour. If I had been smarter, I would have broken up with her right then and there."

Just talking about it again reinforced his embarrassment over the whole affair. Thankfully, he knew Nichole could understand how he'd convinced himself to overlook all of Jill's warning signs. When things were good, they were outstanding. But none of it was worth giving up his self-worth simply to appease someone else's insecurities.

"But I was foolish, or maybe just stubborn, and stuck it out with her for another couple of months. I reasoned with myself that she wasn't someone who appreciated technology. I mean, it's not everyone's cup of tea. Right?"

"So, what was the final straw for you?" Nichole quietly asked.

"It would have been easier to get a text message, but I saw a video on social media of her making out with another guy in a club. I had to take an overnight business trip, and she told me that she would spend a quiet evening at her girlfriend's condo. One of her other girlfriends posted the video online and tagged her on it. Of course, it came up on my newsfeed.

"I could hardly believe my eyes. But the evidence was right there and impossible to deny. When I confronted her about it the next day, she tried to say that it was an old video. And I was dumb enough to believe it, but something kept bugging me about it.

"Luckily, I was smart enough to download a copy of the video before her friend took it down. I sent it to one of my friends and asked him to retrieve the original metadata and enhance the low-light footage to see it better.

"I know it makes me sound like the crazy one to go to so much trouble. Maybe I was a little nutty by then. But Jill drove me to it with her bipolar episodes. My suspicions proved correct when Stephen called me later that week.

"He verified that the posting date coincided with the filming date. Plus, I could clearly see in the enhanced footage that Jill was wearing a necklace that I gave her only the week before. So, not only had she cheated on me, but she also lied about it. Both of those were grounds for ending things. I broke up with her the next day. In-person, in case you were wondering."

"Wow. It sounds like Jill would be a perfect match for Jaxson. We should introduce them to one another." Nichole covered her mouth, unsuccessfully trying to smother a chuckle.

Markson laughed outright. Enough time had passed that he could find the humor in it now. He'd probably dodged a bullet because of Jill's friend. "You know, her friend posted that on purpose."

"What kind of a friend does that?" Nichole shook her head, trying to figure out why.

"The kind who hit on me only a week after Jill and I broke up. Maybe she thought if I wasn't with Jill, then she had a chance with me. I moved the next month and changed my phone number.

"I couldn't deal with that kind of crazy. Plus, I didn't want any of that partying group to affect my career. I'd worked too hard to get where I am. Sometimes, I can be a little slow on the uptake, but I'm not a fool. And I won't make the same mistake twice."

Nichole gave his hand a gentle squeeze. "You were right to end things and to steer clear of them all. Speaking of your career, how long have you been a corporate pilot?"

Markson inwardly cringed. She'd given him the perfect opening to tell her the whole truth, but he couldn't make himself go there. Instead, he focused only on answering her question. "I got my pilot's license as soon as I turned eighteen. But I didn't start flying jets until my college friends got me into it. Richard hooked me up with the jets I fly since he owns the manufacturing company."

"Well, I don't think much of Richard's company since the jet crashed." Nichole pulled her hand away to brush her hair from her face and to swat at an annoying mosquito.

"You should be happy we were flying his jet. Remember, we walked away from the crash without any injury. How many other crash survivors can say the same?" He hated hearing anyone say something against his friend's company. Richard's jets were some of the finest manufactured in the world.

"Okay. You've got me there. But then I was dumb enough to get hurt walking off the edge of a cliff. Go figure, huh? We should try to get some sleep. I'm hoping the rest will help me feel well enough to keep going in the morning."

Panic rushed through Markson's veins. As long as they were talking, he could pretend that danger didn't exist around them. Now, Nichole wanted to change his status quo. He tried to think of some way to keep her awake, even though he knew she needed the rest.

"The ground isn't very comfortable. I doubt we'll get much sleep." His tailbone already ached from sitting on the hard-packed dirt.

"Well, if you want to make it more comfortable for both of us, then you can gather pine needles and pile them up over here. We don't want them too close to the fire, but they're quite comfortable and fragrant if you get enough of them together."

"Why didn't you say something while I was gathering firewood?" Markson shrugged out of the thermal blanket and stood. The cold night air hit his bare chest, causing chill bumps to cover his torso. The fastest way to get warm would be to keep moving.

Scanning the forest behind him, he tried to recall where he'd seen the most needles. Picking a direction, he rushed to complete this new task. If only the rest they'd already had were enough for them to keep going, then he wouldn't be worrying about falling asleep.

Nichole must feel worse than she'd let on. She didn't seem like the type to milk a situation. Besides, she wanted to see her father more than she wanted to sleep in the woods with a stranger.

After about a dozen trips with arms loaded, he managed to bring enough bedding to satisfy Nichole's exacting standard. Initially, he'd tried to create two sleeping spots, but Nichole quickly disabused him of that notion.

"Don't be silly. We've only got one blanket, and it makes more sense for us to share our body heat. It's late, and you'll thank me in the morning." Nichole smiled as she patted the needles next to where she'd created a nest for herself.

Markson looked away from where she lay to scan their perimeter. "Aren't you concerned about bears or something?"

"You worry too much. Unless you have fresh fish or sweets in that bag, any bear will steer clear of our fire. Now, lie down so I can get some sleep. I sure hope you don't snore because I'm a light sleeper." She rolled onto her side, facing away from him.

Feeling self-conscious, Markson kneeled behind Nichole. He spent some more time fiddling with the bedding before finally relenting. A portion of the thermal blanket covered the needles, making it a little less scratchy on his torso, but he didn't hold out much hope for getting any rest. Plus, if he didn't fall asleep, Nichole wouldn't have to worry about whether or not he snored.

Nichole shifted to find out what he was doing, and her elbow brushed against Markson's arm. "Good grief! You're freezing. Put your arm over me and spoon me. We'll get you warm in no time at all." She grabbed his hand and pulled it over her, forcing Markson to comply or sprawl inelegantly on top of her.

Lying behind her, he wondered how this had happened. If his friend had intended to set him up on a blind date, he never would have thought it would end with them sleeping together—even if it were only for basic survival. Nothing could have prepared him for the strange events of the day, but he wondered if his life had forever changed direction because of it.

Nichole's breathing evened out, and she radiated heat almost hotter than their fire. At first self-conscious and more than a little bit nervous, he inhaled softly to keep himself calm. With each breath, he smelled Nichole's strawberry shampoo mixed with campfire smoke.

Minute after minute passed uneventfully. Markson relaxed as Nichole's warmth spread through his whole body, and he was surprisingly comfortable with her cuddled against him. Even though he didn't plan it, he did fall asleep. Deeply and peacefully.

CHAPTER 10
NICHOLE

Heat enveloped Nichole, practically smothering her. Something heavy had draped itself over her torso, causing panic to rise inside her chest as she tried to place where she was. Maybe she was experiencing an incredibly vivid dream. She inhaled cold air laced with a sharp pine tang. When she opened her eyes to the clear, blue sky and her hand felt the pine needles piled underneath her, she remembered everything.

If only this could have been a regular camping trip, yet nothing ordinary or straightforward happened to her lately. Twisting her neck around, she had a clear view of Mark. Another loud snore accosted her ears, making her wonder how she'd slept through that racket. She must have needed the sleep more than she realized.

Which then reminded her of why they were sleeping at all. More than a little apprehensive, she began to bend her knee to test for pain. Immediately, she hissed and regretted it. So much for a good night's rest making things better.

They were no better off than before, maybe worse, actually. Her knee had swollen overnight, indicating more injury than she anticipated. If they'd kept walking last night, then perhaps they would have reached help. Instead, she hurt more now than she had then.

Leveraging herself up on an elbow, made more difficult by the dead weight of Mark's arm, she discovered their fire had burned out. Not much smoke rose, which indicated it had been out for quite some time. "That's not good," she muttered.

Craning her neck to see over Mark's side, she scanned their small campsite, revealing another surprise. They hadn't slept undisturbed by wildlife. Mark's bag no longer resembled anything useful. Most likely, a raccoon or two had visited their camp and spent a considerable amount of time investigating the emergency kit's contents.

Using her elbow, she jabbed it into Mark's side. "Wake up! It's daylight, and we've got a problem."

Mark looked just as confused as she'd felt upon waking. She almost smiled, but now was not the right time for humor. They had to investigate their surroundings to make sure no other animals had come calling. She'd do it herself if she thought she could walk, but that seemed unlikely.

Squinting against the daylight, Markson peered up at Nichole. "What? Oh, hey! Good morning." He quickly removed his arm from over her as if he just realized it wasn't his place.

She already missed their closeness and the heat he provided. A shiver ran through her, but she had to get Mark moving. "You might not say that once you open your eyes. We had visitors last night." She jutted out her jaw toward their camp.

Markson's eyes widened, and he froze mid-breath. "Is there something behind me right now? Should I move slowly?"

This time Nichole did giggle. Mark's reaction was so dramatic; she couldn't contain herself. "I'm sorry, it's not funny. But you should see your expression. No, I can't see any bears, but something tore your bag to shreds. Can you walk the perimeter to make sure nothing is lurking?"

He sat up, the thin blanket noisily crinkling as he pushed it away angrily. He ran his hands roughly over his face and through his hair, making him look crazed as his hair stuck out in every direction when he finished.

"Are you kidding me? I don't have a gun. What would I do if there were something? We just need to get away from here as fast as we can. I'll carry you if you can't walk. Jeez, I feel like we're sitting bait for every carnivore out here." His eyes darted between Nichole and the forest's edge as if he expected something to jump out and attack them at any moment.

Nichole managed to stifle her giggles enough to reply. "I don't think it's that bad. Besides, if there were a bear, we would smell it. They stink, you know. Anyway, we're going to have to figure out what we're going to do for travel today."

She lightly rubbed her thigh, trying to ascertain the extent of the pain. "My knee feels worse today than it did last night. I don't think I'm going to be walking on my own, or very fast even with your assistance. And we can't risk you injuring yourself by trying to carry me."

Markson ran his hands through his hair again, not improving his porcupine impression. He looked as if he were on the edge of panic, trying to process what she said to him. "So what are you suggesting?"

Raising her eyebrows, she lifted her chin to look as strong as possible. This wasn't her ideal solution, but it was quickly becoming their safest course. "You're going to have to leave me here and bring help back."

His mouth dropped open, and he stared silently at her for a full two seconds before he practically exploded. He jumped up from their bed and began pacing, his footsteps thudding dully on the hardpacked ground. "Are you kidding me right now? You just admitted that some wild vermin ransacked our camp, and then you want me to leave you alone and defenseless in the middle of the forest. Nope. No way! The way I see it, you have two choices: I'll carry you, or I'll stay with you. You pick."

"Are you going caveman on me? I thought you said that you trusted my judgment when it came to wilderness survival. Besides, we're only about five miles from help. You can traverse that and be back within a couple of hours. I think I can manage to survive that long." She crossed her arms over her chest, jutting her chin out defiantly. Her eyes narrowed, almost daring him to defy her logic.

"You're forgetting one crucial detail." Markson whipped around on his heel, kneeled in front of her, and stared intently at her.

Nichole had never seen him look so intense, not even during the airplane crash. What had she overlooked? "Oh? What's that?" She had no idea how he could come up with another problem when it all seemed so simple in her mind.

"I have absolutely no idea where we are. If I left you here, I'd have no way of knowing how to get help back to you. As you so aptly put it, I'm a city slicker, hopelessly out of my element here.

"Now, if the roles were reversed, I'd have every confidence that *you* could do exactly as you've asked me to do, but I'm sorry to disappoint you in saying I don't think I could do the same."

Nichole's certainty faltered with each of his words dropping truth bombs on her. She could tell it hurt him to have to admit his shortcomings, but he was right. She could get help. Easily. "Well, I'll come up with something. Let me think about it for a minute. You check our perimeter, and I'll start picking up the mess here."

Markson growled and rose in a burst of frustration. Nichole watched as he stomped away from their small clearing. She hoped he didn't venture too far into the woods; he only needed to walk quietly and observe the woods around them.

At least with his angry, stomping steps, he'd surely scare any curious animal away. There was that benefit to his suddenly volatile mood change. Nichole understood his fear; she could recall a time when she'd gotten lost as a ten-year-old. It must be even more frustrating for him being a grown man. He took his protector role very seriously, but he had to rely on her for direction. That had to grate his pride for someone like him.

She scooted herself across the ground, gritting her teeth against the painful jarring motion, gathering pieces of fabric and tools as she went. Spying the pawprints of multiple raccoons confirmed her initial suspicion. By the time she got to where they'd left the bag, she spotted a pile of raccoon droppings almost touching an object she didn't recall seeing the night before. Careful to avoid contacting the nasty deposit, she picked up the unknown item, turned it over, and realized it was most likely a radio of some sort. "Mark! What's this?"

His crashing footsteps warned her of his approach even before she could spot him. "What's wrong? Are you okay?" His eyes scanned the clearing to his credit before coming to rest on where Nichole sat holding the device.

"Where did you get that?" His voice rose a full octave, and his stride lengthened until he ran toward her. Falling to his knees, he slid across the ground until he stopped just inches from her. Grabbing the device from her, his eyes widened with relief as he clutched it to his chest before holding it out again and shaking it toward her. "Do you know what this is?"

She shook her head, baffled and hopeful because of his sudden intensity. "No. But it looks like an old radio of some sort. Can we call for help with it?"

Markson laughed with a tinge of hysteria. "This isn't a radio—it's even better! It's a satellite phone. We don't have to go anywhere since we can call for help right here. We're saved, Nichole. Oh, I could kiss you right now. I can't believe you found this. Where was it?"

A thrill ran through her at his mention of kissing her, and she felt her cheeks heat. If only he'd follow through and not overthink it. Focusing back to his question, she pointed next to her. "Right here. Do you mean to tell me you had a sat-phone this whole time and you're just now remembering it?"

Her anger flared. If they'd called for help right after running away from that crazy guy, she wouldn't have gotten injured, and she could have been at her father's side yesterday. All of this had been a colossal waste of time, energy, and effort because he forgot he had a solution.

"What? No! I don't know how it got into the bag. I ordered it months ago, but it wasn't in stock. The mechanic or the office assistant must have put it in the emergency kit and forgot to tell me about it. But, whoever did it, I'm going to make sure they get a raise. This is incredible. Just incredible." He clutched it in both of his hands, a goofy grin transforming his expression and making him look just like a little boy with his favorite toy.

Nichole had to content herself with his answer, but it didn't solve their current problem. She'd reserve her hope until she knew help was on its way. "Well, it's not going to do us any good unless you use it. Hopefully, the battery won't be dead like your flashlight last night. What are you waiting for?"

A trace of fear crossed his expression. "Oh, you're right. Okay. Let me see how this works." He held it out and began fiddling with the antenna and a button on the side.

Seeing his indecision didn't inspire much confidence. "Do you even know how that works? Have you used one before?"

He glanced up at her, one eyebrow quirking up playfully. "Nope. But I watched a video about it. I don't think the signal is good enough right here. I'll be right back." Dust rose from where he scrambled to get to his feet.

Nichole shook her head in dismay, waving the cloud of dirt away from her face. She could hardly believe she had to trust her life to this city slicker—him and his videos. What had people ever done before video creations covering nearly every subject?

Watching Mark holding the device in the air reminded her of his stance the day before with the cell phone. Only this time, the sun glinted off of every rippling muscle covering his torso. He didn't appear to have any notion of how his physique affected her, or maybe she hid her reaction well enough. She tore her eyes away from him, not wanting to risk getting caught staring again.

She'd be amused by this apparent groundhog day feeling, but she needed a better outcome than they'd had yesterday. Her incapacitation made their situation much worse. She didn't have a plan B, even if she'd given Mark the impression that she did. This had to work.

CHAPTER 11

MARKSON

Markson wracked his brain to recall the instructional video. If only his assistant had told him the phone had arrived, he would have practiced with it. Goodness, he would have figured it out the day before if he knew he carried it this whole time. He felt stupid for admitting to Nichole that he didn't know about it being in the bag.

He almost whooped in relief with the phone powered up effortlessly. The battery display showed a full charge. Now, all he had to do was get a call locked onto an overhead satellite. So intent had he become watching the phone, he tripped and almost fell over a clump of grass in the meadow.

His foot came down hard, slipping on something squishy. He looked down, seeing a greenish-brown smear of nearly fresh dung. The smell rose to confirm he'd managed to find another sign of wildlife, yet he'd rather have spotted it first than step in it. Yet, if this call could go through, he wouldn't have to worry about it for long.

A glance back toward camp assured Markson that Nichole hadn't witnessed his latest misfortune. She didn't need any more proof of his ineptitude. He needed to redeem himself in her eyes. This phone might give him that opportunity as soon as he could get it to work.

The screen displayed a lock. Markson restrained his whoop of delight and brought it down to tap in the numbers for his office. The ring sounded distant and tinny, but it was music to his ears.

"Rothschild Capital Ventures. This is Brittney. How may I direct your call?"

"Brittney, thank goodness. This is Markson. We've had a plane crash, and I need you to route my helicopter to pick us up." Markson had no idea how long the call would stay connected. He hoped it would be enough.

"Mr. Rothschild! Are you or your passenger hurt? Do you need medical attention? What is your location?"

He could hear her tapping out the helicopter order on the keyboard even as she asked her questions. Thank goodness Brittney had a good head on her shoulders. "I'm fine. Nichole sprained her knee last night after the crash. We'll need clearance to land at the hospital heliport in Gatlinburg. I don't know our location. Does this sat-phone have a way to display coordinates?"

"One moment; I'll look that up." Another furious round of keyboard clacking and a moment's silence passed before Brittney gave the instructions to extract their GPS location coordinates. "Okay, I got it. The helicopter is already en route, and I'll relay these coordinates to him right now. I'm glad you're okay, Mr. Rothschild. I'll contact insurance to let them know about the plane and set in motion the recovery effort."

"Thanks, Brittney. There might be a problem with recovery. Have the insurance adjuster call me before they send anyone out there. We'll probably have to get the local law enforcement involved. I'll explain later.

"Let the pilot know we're right next to a clear, big meadow. He'll have a perfect place to land without obstruction."

"Will do. Have a safe flight, sir."

Markson made his way back to camp with a jaunt to his step, careful to avoid any more animal droppings. The phone swung by his side, clutched tightly in his hand, making him even more grateful that he'd had the foresight to buy it. Finally, he'd done something to help their situation.

Then the reality of his situation hit him like a prize fighter's punch to the gut; as soon as the helicopter arrived, he wouldn't have any excuse to stay in Nichole's company anymore. If he planned to have any kind of future relationship with her, he'd have to do something to ensure it. His one-hour time limit was already running.

"Great news. It worked, and help is on its way!" he called out as soon as he got close enough to see her reaction. He held the phone over his head, pumping it victoriously as he had with his Heisman trophy.

Nichole immediately perked up, her face brightening at the news. "What kind of help? How soon will they get here?"

"A helicopter is coming and can land right out there. I can carry you to it. It should be here in about an hour. That should give us just enough time to break camp and gather our things. We wouldn't want to leave any trace of our passing. Would we?" He plopped down onto the ground next to her, grinning so wide it hurt his cheeks.

Nichole cocked her head, her hand hovering just above his as they both went to pick up the first-aid kit. "I don't understand why the authorities would take so long to get here. It's not like they have that far to go. That is who you called, right?"

Markson shook his head. "No, I contacted my company. It was the first place I thought to call. I wanted them to know we survived. When I failed to check in to my final destination, I'm sure it caused quite a stir.

"Plus, I didn't know if I'd get more than one call from the phone. Brittney arranged the helicopter pick-up. And, she even walked me through how to get GPS coordinates from this." He held up the sat-phone, still thrilled to discover it had made it with them on this ill-begotten flight.

Markson paused to stare at Nichole. How could he convince her of his sincerity to get to know her better? What if she didn't want to keep in touch after he brought her to Gatlinburg? He couldn't stomach the idea of losing contact with her. He didn't like that idea at all. "Nichole, I'm glad I got to know you. I wanted to talk to you about something."

She exhaled quickly out of her nostrils. Her fingers plucked at the blades of grass next to her. "Is that your way of telling me goodbye?"

"No!" He could tell his response came out a bit too abruptly when Nichole jumped and her eyes snapped up to meet his. He wasn't doing this right. He had to do better. "I mean, I'd like to stay in touch. When I told you earlier that I'd stay until you told me to go, I meant every word of it. You're different from anyone else I've ever met. I'd like to see where things could go between us."

"You got all that from spending fifteen stress-filled hours with me?" She shook her head, chuckling softly to herself.

Markson had to do something to impress upon her his sincerity. Only one thing came to mind. If he had more time, he would've come up with any number of romantic gestures to pique her interest. But time was the enemy here. And what he felt for Nichole even surprised him. He reached over and put his hands on either side of her face, turning her so she had to look at him. "Yes."

Her breath caught, and her eyes immediately shifted to his lips. That was what he'd hoped she'd do. He slowly leaned forward until the barest breath of space lingered between them. He'd leave it up to her to kiss him or turn away.

Her eyelids fluttered closed. Markson almost groaned in the agony of defeat, but then her lips touched his. Immediately, his hands moved into her hair, but he had to remind himself to remain gentle. He didn't want to scare her away. She wasn't like the girls he knew; she was scarred and tender.

Markson pressed his lips to hers just to let her know this wasn't just a friendly kiss. He wished he could do more, but this wasn't the time or the place. Patience wasn't usually his strong suit, but their uninterrupted time together was quickly ending. Hopefully, this kiss let her know exactly how he felt about her.

Fighting every instinct inside him, he ended the kiss and pulled away. His hands trailed from Nichole's hair and down her shoulders until they reached her hands. He gave them a gentle squeeze and waited for her to make the next move.

When Nichole didn't say anything more and kept her eyes cast down to where he touched her, he gave her hands a gentle squeeze and let go. "I'll start dismantling camp. But promise me that you'll think about what I said." He had to content himself with the merest nod of her head. She obviously needed time to process what just happened between them.

With more enthusiasm than he felt, he swooped down and grabbed a massive armload of the organic bedding they'd shared. By the fourth trip, Markson never wanted to see another pine needle as long as he lived. After carrying the last load and dumping it back under the tree, his whole torso itched abominably, and he smelled like a Christmas tree. Although, that aspect probably improved his scent since he hadn't bathed in more than twenty-four hours.

As he'd done numerous times already, he turned his forearm and checked his watch. Time hadn't exactly sped by, but he imagined the helicopter must be getting close. The echoes through mountains the night before led him to believe they'd hear the aircraft long before they saw it.

He returned to where Nichole remained seated and picked a grassy patch to join her. "It should be here any time now." He looked at his watch again. "It's been an hour."

Nichole grabbed his wrist and hauled it closer to herself. After making a strange scoffing sound, she said, "That's a pretty fancy watch, Mark."

Suddenly self-conscious, Markson pulled his arm out of her grasp. He should tell her the truth, but he still couldn't force himself to admit anything. Not yet. "It's a perk of the job. I have to be on time, you know."

"A Rolex is a pretty nice perk. I didn't realize that about corporate pilots." Her eyes drilled into his, almost daring him to correct her statement.

Had she figured out his secret? How was he supposed to respond to that comment? He opened and closed his mouth twice, still trying to come up with a rebuttal. Thankfully, movement in his peripheral vision distracted him. Turning his head, he spotted the helicopter clearing the mountain they'd descended the night before. Pointing like a little kid, he exclaimed unnecessarily, "There it is! I'm going to make sure he knows where we are."

Markson leaped to his feet and ran full out into the clearing, arms waving over his head. He didn't care if he looked foolish; he simply wanted to get Nichole to the hospital as fast as he could. Or, maybe avoid any more awkward questions if he were honest with himself. Seeing the slight shift in the helicopter's flight path, Markson knew the pilot had spotted him.

Markson made a complete circle inspecting the ground for obstructions and loose debris. A field landing could be dangerous. The last thing he wanted was another downed aircraft in his fleet because of something so preventable.

Finding the perfect landing spot closer to their camp, Markson trampled the ground, flattening as much of the tall grass as he could. He flung several limbs away along with a couple of rocks. The helicopter rotors sounded close; he glanced up to see the pilot waiting for him to indicate it was time to land.

Giving the pilot a thumbs-up gesture, he jogged out of the circle. Turning his back, he felt grass and small clumps of dirt pelting his bare skin—definitely not ideal to be shirtless at a time like this. He moved a little farther away until he heard the rotors idling down.

Rushing back toward the aircraft, Markson opened the passenger door and leaned into the cockpit's shelter. Markson should have guessed that Jenkins would pilot this mission, and he knew the man's trustworthiness. Raising his voice over the sound of the engine, he said, "Nichole's injured. Sprained knee. She doesn't know who I am, and I'd like to keep it that way. Do you have clearance to land at the Gatlinburg hospital?"

Jenkins nodded. "Yes, sir. Once you're both on board, we can be there in about five minutes. I'll call it in as soon as we're airborne. I'm glad to see you're okay, Mr. Rothschild."

Markson mirrored Jenkins' grin. "Me, too. I'll be right back." Markson didn't wait for an answer before slamming the door and rushing back to their dismantled camp. He probably wouldn't have been able to find it again had Nichole not been seated in plain sight.

CHAPTER 12
NICHOLE

What was she supposed to say to Mark, now that she kissed him? Was that his intention when he stayed so close to her? Or had she simply read into the situation what she wanted? He'd said all the right things afterward, but maybe he was just trying to be nice to her. She didn't know why she was putting so much effort into trying to figure him out. Once they got to Gatlinburg, she'd probably never see him again.

Besides, something didn't seem quite right with him. It almost felt like he was keeping something from her. Nichole couldn't shake the feeling that she forgot something. Any progress she might have made disintegrated the moment Mark turned and raced toward her from the helicopter.

She didn't bother trying to hide the fact that she was staring at him and enjoying the show; she couldn't stop herself even if someone paid her. When he kneeled in front of her, his chest barely heaved. Her eyes remained focused on his chest, and it took her a second to register that Mark had spoken. "What was that?"

He quirked an eyebrow. "I know I'm a bit distracting, but if I could bother to interrupt your thoughts, we've got to get moving. Can you hold the emergency supplies while I carry you?"

Embarrassment washed over her. Her cheeks burned with as much heat as the campfire's flames the night before. He so effortlessly called her out for staring at him. Any distraction was welcome at this point. She looked over the pile of items, and an idea came to her. "We can wrap everything in the thermal blanket. That should help keep things contained so that I won't drop anything." At least that sounded halfway intelligent.

"Good idea." Markson's eyes sparkled with mischief, but he grabbed the folded foil blanket and unfurled it. Together they heaped the items on it, and Markson pulled the corners together. He held it out to Nichole.

Her grin matched his while she reached over to take the bundle. Electricity sparked from him and into her hand as her fingers brushed against his. She jerked her hand back, nervously giggled, and then returned to receive the bag. "That was shocking."

"Sorry. Are you ready now?" He held out his arms, clearly intending to pick her up as soon as she permitted him.

"Yep, all set." She nodded, clutching the supplies tight to her chest. It was one thing that he carried her when she was tired and in pain; it was quite another for her to be well-rested and clear-headed enough to appreciate his strength.

More than anything, she wished she could spread her hands over his chest and feel the play of muscles under his smooth skin. Instead, she had to content herself with the feel of his arms holding her close to him. She breathed deeply, mostly trying to clear her head of such wayward thoughts, but ended up inhaling the pine scent covering him. So much for clearing her mind.

Looking away, she focused her attention on the enormous aircraft waiting for them. From their camp, it didn't look nearly as large. "What kind of helicopter is that?" She had to raise her voice as they closed the distance.

He practically beamed at her question. "It's a Sikorsky. It's fast and has a comfortable flight. You'll have an entire bank of seats you can lie on so you won't have to bend your knee."

Inwardly, she smiled at his enthusiasm. He acted as if he owned the helicopter rather than the company he worked for. His appreciation for aviation must span all aircraft and not just jets. Or, he could be like any red-blooded male and simply enjoyed any motorized vehicle that went fast.

Even with the rotor blades rotating slower while at idle, debris still flew wildly through the air. Nichole turned her face into Markson's chest to protect herself from the stinging onslaught, closing her eyes tightly and hoping her body provided enough of a shield so Markson didn't get hurt. Guilt ravaged her because she still wore his shirt wrapped around her knee; she should have given it back.

But then she would have given up her eye candy. The random thought made her grin. Another truth raced on its heels that she'd lose the one tie she had with him. As long as she kept his shirt, she had an excuse to see him again. Not that he'd care about an ordinary article of clothing, but it gave her hope.

Markson struggled to open the door while still holding her. Nichole belatedly realized what was going on when she opened her eyes and immediately reached out to help. Together, they got the door opened, and she pulled herself onto the bank of seats.

She had no idea helicopters could be this large as well as this luxurious. She'd only ever heard about millionaires having aircraft such as this. Nichole looked around the cabin with her mouth gaping. She missed Mark getting into the helicopter but quickly noticed the difference as soon as he closed the door and sealed them inside. "This thing must seat a dozen people!"

Mark grinned at her, nodding and leaning forward so she could hear him better, "A baker's dozen, actually! Do you need me to help you buckle up?" He extended his hands toward her middle as if to put action to his question.

Acting before thinking, she shook her head and began feeling under her for the straps. "No, I've got it. Thanks." If she had been thinking, she would have let him. Not only would it have been faster and possibly less painful, but she would also have had a valid excuse for him to be close again. She could have kicked her stupid, independent streak for causing her another missed opportunity.

While she fiddled with the belt, she noticed Mark talking with the pilot. She didn't hear what they said, but she imagined it had to do with their readiness to fly. As soon as she fastened the buckle, the noise from the rotors overhead increased. A few seconds later, they lifted from the field and tilted slightly forward as they gained altitude and speed at an incredible rate.

Nichole watched the ground fall away. As soon as they rose higher than the next mountain, she had a clear view of the nearby city. She'd been right that they were close. It soothed her pride that she'd been leading them in the right direction—not that she'd had any doubt.

Her attention was split between the scenery whizzing below and the still, half-naked man seated across from her. His intense stare made her self-conscious but also curious. What was he thinking? Did he really want to stay in touch? If so, why? What was in it for him?

It wasn't as if she'd given him any reason to want to stay. As far as she was concerned, she'd brought him nothing but trouble. Besides, her life wasn't exactly ready for another change. Being back home and caring for her father was going to be a full-time job.

The helicopter's direction shifted, and the aircraft banked to give Nichole a better view out her window. As often as she'd flown into the Gatlinburg airport, she'd never come from this direction or this low over the sprawling town. The rescue flight only lasted a few minutes, as promised, and she realized they were landing at the LeConte Medical

Center—the same place where her dad had checked himself into the day before.

Tears of joy sprang to her eyes. She wouldn't have long to wait before finding out how her dad was doing while she got herself checked out. This rescue couldn't have worked out any better. Well, if they'd known about the sat-phone, this flight could have happened the evening before, but she wasn't going to split hairs about it now.

The pilot's skill showed when she didn't even notice the helicopter touching down to the ground. The change in the rotor noise was her first indication, followed almost instantly by Mark unbuckling himself and reaching for the door handle.

Without consciously trying to go into her nurse mode, Nichole spotted the angry red color of Mark's outstretched hand, and she gasped. "Mark! Look at your hand. You have to come into the hospital with me."

Almost comically, Markson's expression changed to wonder as he turned his hand over and scrutinized it. "Huh. I guess I'll have to. Now, let's see about getting you inside, shall we?"

She'd been so concerned about his hand that she forgot about her seat belt. Markson flipped the lever with practiced ease, and the pressure left her waist. Before she could form any protest, Markson had her back in his arms, and he stepped out of the helicopter as if she didn't weigh anything. Hunching over her as he jogged away from the swirl of the overhead blades, she allowed herself the moment to appreciate the play of his muscles even as she tried to ignore the jarring pain of her knee.

She'd hoped to stay longer in his arms, but the hospital staff must have known about their arrival. Mark hadn't even made it to the protective fencing enclosing the helipad before they had a gurney rolling out to receive her. An instant sensation of loss overwhelmed her as soon as Mark's body no longer touched hers.

How could she have grown so attached to him in such a short amount of time? Yet, the idea of being parted made her feel like panicking. Her breathing hitched, and her palms started to sweat. She was sure if they took her blood pressure just then, it would have been off the charts.

A nurse buckled her in, and the snapping sound mirrored the sound of her heart breaking. A second nurse braced her knee with a rolled blanket before they started moving her along the bumpy sidewalk and away from where Mark stayed behind.

She had to do something before the moment of opportunity passed. Urgently, she grabbed the nurse's arm and said, "Wait! Mark needs to see someone for his hand."

"Oh? We hadn't heard anything about a second patient. I'll take a look at his condition. I'll see you inside." The woman patted her hand and turned back the way they'd come.

Nichole watched helplessly as the distance between them increased. What if Mark refused treatment and got back into the helicopter? She didn't have any way to get in touch with him again. She couldn't hear whatever the nurse said, but Mark nodded and turned away. The last thing Nichole saw before the exterior doors snapped shut was Mark stepping into the helicopter and the nurse returning without him.

A tear of pain and frustration dripped from her eye. Annoyed that she'd let herself get so wrapped up in Mark, she brusquely wiped it away. She couldn't focus on what that man did right now; she had to find out about her dad.

Shifting her attention back to the nurse pushing the gurney, she said, "My dad said he was checking himself in yesterday for a possible MCI. Can you give me an update on his condition?" She hoped by using the medical term for a heart attack would lend some credibility to her request.

"Oh? What's his name? I was on duty yesterday, and it was pretty slow."

Nichole had used that same expression of professionalism and compassion with her patients. Hopefully, she'd get a break in her streak of bad luck. "Jacob Monroe."

Immediately the nurse smiled compassionately. "He's your dad? Oh, he was nice."

Thankfully she was already sitting as one word stuck out. She felt faint as she whispered, "Was? What are you saying?"

The nurse patted her arm affectionately. "Oh, honey, not that! He was cleared and sent home last night. I can give him a call for you while we're waiting for your doctor to be ready to see you. Would you like that?"

"Yes! Please. My phone died, and our plane crashed. I tried so hard to get here, and I worried I'd be too late again. Oh, thank you so much." Nichole snapped her mouth shut before she could babble more than she already had. Her father was okay; he hadn't died. In only a few more minutes, she'd hear his voice, and everything would be alright. She felt like she could breathe easily again.

The nurse wheeled the gurney through the emergency room and into a private section to the right. She asked Nichole the usual medical questions and filled out the paperwork. Getting changed into the hospital gown proved difficult and painful, but the nurse's help made it possible. Several minutes later, the nurse left her alone, pulling the fabric divider closed again and leaving Nichole to nothing but her thoughts and the prospect of developing hypothermia.

Rolling onto her back, she breathed deeply and exhaled slowly, suppressing shivers that only made her knee hurt worse. It was true that medical professionals were the worst patients. She knew what needed to happen, but waiting for doctors, labs, or x-rays was by far the most frustrating part about being injured.

Time became her enemy. Thinking allowed her to recall the fantastic adventure she'd shared with a stranger. She no longer had to worry about her father's health. A second problem quickly replaced her primary one. What was she supposed to do about Mark?

CHAPTER 13

MARKSON

Markson pulled the helicopter door shut behind him so he could speak without shouting. Sitting in the co-pilot's seat, Markson said, "Hey, Jenkins, I'm going to get my hand checked out." He displayed his palm for Jenkins to see. Markson glanced down offhandedly, only then noticing the angry red lines showing on his wrist.

Hmm, that doesn't look good. Maybe Nichole's right to be concerned.

In a more distracted tone, he added, "And then I need to take care of a few things while I'm in Gatlinburg. It might take a couple of days. Feel free to stay here or go back home to Atlanta. You know the drill."

Jenkins nodded before looking pointedly at Markson's hand. "That looks pretty serious. I'm glad you're having it looked at. I think I'll stay, boss. I've always wanted to visit Dollywood. Maybe, I'll even luck out and see Dolly herself.

I'll keep my cell charged and ready. Let me know when you need me back."

"Hey, speaking of cell phones. Mine's dead since I had to leave my charger inside the jet. It's a long story, but a man shot at us and chased us away from the wreckage. It's going to be interesting trying to recover the plane. Can you let Brittney know—?"

"I've got just what you need." Jenkins pulled his flight bag out from beside his seat up into his lap. After digging for a couple of seconds, he pulled out a charging cord and a portable, rechargeable battery pack. "I never fly without extra insurance."

Jenkins didn't know it, but he'd just earned himself a huge bonus for his selfless generosity. Markson gratefully received the items. "Thanks. You just saved me a lot of headaches. Now, I'll be able to call Brittney myself."

Jenkins squirmed and looked distinctly uncomfortable.

"Was there something else, Jenkins?"

"Um, yeah. Would you like my shirt, too? I wasn't going to say anything, but it looks like something happened to yours."

Jenkins's unexpected question seemed to unlock his pent-up tension. Laughter echoed through the helicopter. "Thanks, man, but I'll get mine back from Nichole. Besides,

I think she likes me walking around like this. I do what I can to keep the ladies happy." Man, it felt good to laugh. He reached for the door latch. "Thanks again for rescuing us. Nice flying."

He hopped from the helicopter, ducking low as he ran until he reached the safe area beyond the fence. Before he faced his uncertain fate inside the hospital, he pulled his dead phone from his pocket and started it charging.

Hopefully, by the time he got his hand situated, he'd have enough charge to get some much-needed business done. He'd been keeping a running list of items that required immediate attention—most of which involved Nichole's family business. It would be nice to clear some of those tasks to concentrate on more important matters—namely, Nichole.

Feeling like he'd done as much as he could, he waved to Jenkins as the helicopter lifted. At least Jenkins only had a short, two-minute flight considering Markson could see from where he stood the airport just beyond the fence and a field. Hopefully, the airport would have a courtesy car for Jenkins to use on his mini-vacation. The guy deserved it, plus so much more. He looked forward to surprising his devoted employee with something outlandish.

He'd stalled long enough, time to face the doctors. As much as he respected the profession, he wished they could do their job with fewer needles and a lot less pain. Markson's previous experience made him leery, but the look of his hand concerned him more than a little bit.

The nurse who he'd seen outside waited for him just inside the sliding doors. He should have known she wouldn't go far. Only two steps into the hospital, and she held out a hospital gown for him. Hiding a grin, he nodded his thanks and slung his arms into the holes, and left it open at the front.

After looking him up and down, the nurse said, "Right this way, sir." She was all business and not in the least affected by his style of dressing. "We'll need to get your insurance information and have you fill out some paperwork. Will you need help with that?"

"I'll be paying with cash, and I'm right-handed, so help would be much appreciated."

"Take a seat in here. I'll send in a medical assistant to get your paperwork done."

The curtain hadn't even stopped moving before a young girl about twenty entered armed with a clipboard and a stethoscope. "Hi, I'm Emily. How are you feeling today?"

Markson waited for the usual reaction when the girl finally looked up to see him. Yep, there it was. Her cheeks flushed, and she looked away quickly. "I've been better." He flashed her a glimpse of his puffy hand. "How are you? Has it been a busy shift for you today?"

"Oh, I'm good. I love it when it's busy. The day flies by, and I get to meet so many interesting people. Okay, can I get your name?"

"Mark Roth." He didn't even hesitate. It was the pseudonym he used whenever he wanted to maintain his privacy. He continued to give his business mailing address and phone number. His staff already knew what to do with the odd mail or phone call coming into the office.

She finished with the paperwork and set it down next to him on the paper-covered table. "Alright, I need to get your vitals first. Then, I'll remove those dressings and see what the doctor's got to work with on your hand. Sound good?"

Markson nodded. He kept himself from shivering when the girl's cold hands touched his chest, but the chill bumps rose without any warning.

"Sorry, my hands are a bit chilly. Your pulse, heart, and lungs are all good. Now, about the hand. What did you do to it, and how long ago?"

Her hands felt even colder against the fevered skin of his hand. He hadn't realized the progression of the problem until that moment. "Last night, as it was getting dark, I fell down a mountainside and used a bush to slow my descent. I didn't notice then how bad it was. My girlfriend had me wash it in the river right away, and we packed it with wet moss until we could bandage it properly."

"Moss, hmm? That's interesting. Well, you've got yourself quite the gash. I'm going to rinse it with saline solution. It shouldn't sting too much."

Markson didn't particularly want a running description of what was going to happen. He wished they could knock him out and take care of it as had occurred for his knee, but he wasn't holding out much hope of that. It was a nice fantasy.

He needed something better to occupy his thoughts. Unsurprisingly, Nichole sprang to mind. Yes, she was much better to think about. He wondered where she'd been taken.

Almost as if his thoughts had been broadcast, he heard a girl's voice that sounded suspiciously like Nichole's. As soon as the medical assistant left his cubicle, he jumped off the bench and leaned closer to the side curtain. After hearing her say a few more words, he knew he'd been right.

Knowing he was probably breaking the rules, he called out, "Knock, knock."

"Come in," Nichole called out.

He tweaked the curtain open and looked around the edge. "Howdy, neighbor."

"You stayed!" Nichole sat up so fast she jarred her knee. She hissed and grabbed at her leg, but she didn't take her eyes off him.

"You sound surprised." How could she have thought he'd leave? Had he done the right thing by staying?

"But, I saw you get back into the helicopter."

It angered him to think she'd had a moment of uncertainty concerning him. He should have told her his plans rather than let her worry—another lesson learned the hard way.

"Well, it was easier to get some details taken care of. Don't you remember I told you that I'd stay with you until you told me to leave? I'm a man of my word, and I'm afraid you're stuck with me." He looked around her empty exam room and said, "Who were you talking to?"

"Oh, that was my dad on the phone. He's on his way over."

"That's good. I was worried maybe you were getting delirious from your pain. I can't wait to meet him." This could get tricky. He'd have to play his cards right to get the information he needed to straighten out the mess his intern caused. "I might need my shirt back, though. I doubt your father would appreciate my physique quite the same as you have."

He just couldn't help teasing her. Seeing her blush all over again was reward enough. Two things became evident in the last twenty-four hours. First, there was such a thing as a woman worth fighting for. And, second, Nichole was that woman.

As much as he'd resisted the idea of marriage, he couldn't keep the idea of doing just that with Nichole. He knew it sounded insane, especially considering their short, trying time together. But, if he knew a critical thing about people, their real personalities shone through during the worst of times.

If yesterday were Nichole at her worst, then he could hardly wait to see her at her best. Now, if only he could prove to her that he was worth fighting for. Would she still feel the same way once she found out that he'd ruined her father's life?

Could he blame her if she did decide to shut him out? He didn't want to find out. If the roles were reversed, he'd have a hard time believing his side of the story.

If any of his friends were to tell him this is what love felt like, he would have told them they were crazy. He'd never wanted to protect someone in the same way he tried to with Nichole. And, even stranger, she was the least likely to need any protection, let alone his. Maybe that was the attraction; she didn't need him.

Her independence and her career gave her her self-worth. Every woman who'd thrown herself at him ended up being insecure and shallow. Those were the two traits he despised the most, yet that was all he'd ever encountered. No wonder he'd always been so cynical.

And, no wonder he hadn't thought twice before entering into that pact with his friends never to get married. That turned out not to work so well, considering that four of them had found and married their soulmates. Only he and Stephen remained single. Whoever was last to get married had to pay the other five guys a million dollars each. It sounded so petty to him now, but at the time, it was an amusing lark—something only billionaire bachelors would joke about.

"Mr. Roth? Please take a seat in your cubicle. We need to start working on your hand."

Markson would have gladly sat on the edge of Nichole's gurney had the doctor not taken hold of his arm and guided him away. "Don't leave without me," he said over his shoulder.

NICHOLE

"Dad! It's so good to see you!" Nichole held out her arms, eager to receive a warm hug from the man who had raised her from the time she was three. Tears prickled her eyes as he held her tight. She refused to let him go, even when the shift in position stretched her leg painfully.

"What happened to you?" Jacob said, forcibly removing her arms from around him and moving back until he could see all of her.

"A series of unfortunate events. But that doesn't matter. They're going to take a CT scan of my knee, but I already know that it's just a bad sprain." She didn't want to tell him about the plane crash or the close call with the maniac, not until she assured herself that his heart was strong enough. "Tell me what happened when you went to the emergency room yesterday?"

"Well, that was a colossal waste of time. It turned out only to be heartburn. I guess I shouldn't have hot salsa on an empty stomach. I'm sorry I even worried you about it. I feel like all this," he gestured to her room and then her prone body, "is my fault."

"No, Dad, it wasn't. But, one good thing did come out of all of this." It might be too soon to say anything, but her dad was her best friend. She had to share, or she'd burst. Whispering, she added, "I think I found the man I'm going to marry."

"What's this?"

"Shhh, Dad. Keep your voice down. He's in the next cubicle."

Nichole's grin almost hurt. Her dad's reaction was priceless as he looked in the same direction I had.

"He a doctor? I guess that makes sense, but I thought you didn't like dating doctors. You said they were all egotistical. Well, I look forward to meeting him. Is he the one treating you?"

"Slow down, Dad. You're getting way ahead of me here. No, he's not a doctor. He's another patient. I think you'll like him. He used to play for the NFL—"

"I don't think you'd be happy marrying an athlete. Not after Jaxson—"

Good grief, she didn't want to go there. "I said *used to*, Dad. He's a corporate pilot now. He flew me here. Well, most of the way here anyway."

After catching up with her dad about the previous twenty-four hours, she wilted back onto her pillow. Even talking about it made her tired again. Relief and worry washed through her when the med-tech came to get her for the CT scan.

"Dad? Promise me you'll stay right here until I get back."

"I wasn't planning on going anywhere. Besides, how else were you planning to get home? I'll wait right here."

Time was running out. She knew the CT scanning schedule was tight—they were at every hospital where she'd worked. "You know that's not what I mean. Don't get any ideas about talking with Mark. I want to introduce you. Okay?"

"Okay. Now, get moving."

He never lied to her. She felt good about leaving, but she'd feel better once she got back.

CHAPTER 14

MARKSON

Eavesdropping on Nichole's conversation with her dad proved to be a great distraction. He hardly noticed a thing they did to his hand. After a dozen painful pokes with a needle for local anesthetic, a thorough cleaning, seventeen stitches, and enough gauze to wrap a mummy, his hand was unrecognizable but expected to heal completely.

"The swelling will go down once the antibiotics start working," the doctor said. He stood, gathered his clipboard, and left without another word.

Markson appreciated efficiency, but he thought the doctor could work on his bedside manner. A smile or a friendly word would have made the experience better. But then, he could understand the demands on the doctor's time. Plus, he had somewhere he wanted to go himself.

Scooting off the bench, he grabbed his cell phone and charger and walked the few feet to reach Nichole's cubicle.

He knew she hadn't returned yet. Being able to speak with her father alone was precisely what he wanted. This couldn't have worked out better if he'd planned it.

Walking into the cubicle, he said, "Excuse me. I don't want to intrude, but Nichole had my shirt." He'd spotted it on the chair earlier, but now Jacob sat in that chair, and the shirt was gone.

Jacob jumped up, held out his hand, and then spotted Markson's injured hand. He withdrew his hand and opted to nod in greeting instead. "You must be Mark. I'm Jacob Monroe, Nichole's father."

"Yes, sir. It's a pleasure meeting you. I'm glad to see you're in good health. Nichole was anxious about getting here to see you." He looked away from Jacob to locate his shirt. Spotting it on a rolling tray, he reached across the gurney and grabbed it. "Excuse me while I get dressed. Your daughter absconded with my shirt and left me shivering in the cold for most of the time we spent together. I'm sure she told you all about it."

Markson shrugged out of the hospital gown and then realized how difficult a task it would be to get his bandaged hand down the tight shirt sleeve. He briefly considered ripping the sleeve off but then thought better of it. Staring stupidly at his shirt wasn't exactly the impression he wanted to make on Nichole's father.

"Do you need help with that?"

Markson laughed, turning to face Jacob. "I guess I do."

With Jacob's gentle help, Markson finally got his shirt on. At least the anesthetic was still active, but he hated to think about when he had to take it off again. Maybe a pair of scissors would be on his shopping list.

"Thanks for the help." There didn't seem to be any way to get to the subject without sounding awkward. "So, Nichole tells me that you're recently retired."

Jacob laughed outright. "Recently retired!" A few more chuckles escaped before he nodded. "I guess I am. If you'd call having my business stolen and sold without my permission, then yes."

"Yeah, Nichole mentioned that, as well. I'm sorry. How did you meet your business partner?" He hitched his hip onto the gurney so he could rest his hand across his thigh. Maybe he could learn something useful for trying to locate the thief.

"He started golfing at the same club I attend. We struck up a friendship, and I brought him into my company right after Nichole finished nursing school. It was the perfect arrangement. I still can't believe I misread him so badly. I'm usually an excellent judge of character. He and I are from the same generation, so I thought his word was his bond. It appears he wasn't raised the same."

"Did he ever say where he grew up?"

"No, not anything specific. He mentioned living in the midwest several times, but that could mean anything. Or it could have been a lie. I just don't know anymore. So help me if I ever see Sal again. He's got some nasty karma coming his way."

"I thought I might help you find him. It doesn't seem right that he could sell your company and then steal all the money."

"Oh, I couldn't ask you to do that. It's not your problem."

Markson wished that were the case. This was very much his problem. "You didn't ask. I offered. Plus, I have a friend who enjoys this kind of thing. Let me take a crack at it."

"What's going on here?"

Markson almost gave himself whiplash, turning so fast to see Nichole sitting in a wheelchair at her cubicle entrance. Who knew those wheelchairs could be so quiet? Not that he was trying to go behind her back—well, not much. At least he had a good reason for his subterfuge. He was trying to do the right thing for her family.

Markson moved to make room for Nichole's return to her bed. "Nothing. The doctor finished with my hand, and I came to get my shirt. Your dad was sitting here all alone. We were just getting to know one another."

He needed to shut up before he got himself into more trouble. Nichole's expression looked suspicious enough. Time to move the conversation to something more neutral. "Is there any word when you can get sprung from this place?"

"They're waiting for the CT test results. It's probably going to be another couple of hours. Why?" More than anything, he wanted to pick her up from the chair and gently place her in the bed. But he stayed rooted to where he was, forced to watch helplessly as the med-tech slowly assisted Nichole back onto the bed. Every time she winced, Markson wanted to push the tech away and take charge. But he couldn't do anything but watch, just as her father did the same. Jacob's pained expression probably mirrored his own.

"I'll be back soon," Markson said. He couldn't make his escape fast enough. "I've got some business calls to make." Taking his phone out of his pocket, he saw it had almost a full charge. Perfect. Using only his left hand, he dialed his office.

"Brittney, this is Markson. I need you to do some things for me."

"Sure thing, boss."

"I'm going to be staying in Gatlinburg for at least a week. Find out where Jacob Del Monroe lives and buy a house nearby under Nichole Childress's name. Make sure it is furnished with everything. Do the same thing for a car. I'll use both while I'm here. Text me the new address once you have it."

"As soon as we get off the phone, I'm going to need you to wire transfer money to pay my hospital bill, and I want to cover Nichole Childress's charges, as well."

"Got it. Anything else?"

Thank goodness for an efficient assistant. "Yes, send me all of the documents, including contracts, emails, notes—*everything* on the JDM Manufacturing acquisition. Put a hold on anything related to that deal. Get Peterson in Legal to review every shred of documentation on the transaction and have him call me as soon as he's finished."

"I'll have that in your email within fifteen minutes. Anything else?"

"Since my phone's been dead, I haven't heard from the insurance adjuster about the downed jet. Let them know they'll have to work with the authorities if they plan to recover it. We crashed next to a hermit's cabin, and he took shots at us. He thought we landed a helicopter to take him prisoner. He's not right in the head, and it might not be worth trying to retrieve the plane. Tell them I don't mind taking the hit if they don't want to endanger any of their adjusters while investigating."

"Sounds like you've had quite the adventure. I'm doubly glad you're okay after hearing all of this. Would you like me to order a replacement jet?"

"No, I'll call Richard myself. I might upgrade to his latest model. We'll see."

"Sounds good, boss. Just let me know if you think of anything else you need."

"Oh, find out what kind of truck Jenkins has been dreaming about and have it delivered to his house."

"I already know. He's going to be thrilled. Is he staying in Gatlinburg, as well?"

"Yes." He could hear the excitement in Brittney's voice, and he felt the same thrill. Markson loved that his employees had close relationships outside of work. Jenkins's wife and Brittney were best friends, and the reason Brittney had applied for the job with his company.

Nothing made him happier than surprising his employees with extravagant bonuses. He'd maintained the motto of hiring the best, paying them well, and giving them everything they needed to keep them happy. Not only did he have devoted employees, but he also never had to worry about anyone betraying his trust.

"I'll let Sherri know not to expect him home tonight. Anything else?"

"Ha. That's enough for now. If I think of anything else, I'll shoot you a text message. Thanks for everything. I really appreciate it."

"It's my pleasure. Oh, Boss?"

"Yes?"

"I can't wait to meet Nichole. She must be amazing."

"You have no idea." Markson had no idea how Brittney always did that with him. Not only was she a genuinely gifted assistant, but also a valued asset to his company. He didn't know what he'd do without her.

He planned to spend as much time with Nichole as he could until he got the address to the house. But the idea of watching her leave with her father bothered him. If only he could convince the two of them to go somewhere with him. Unfortunately, that wasn't on the table; they would both find his invitation more than a little strange.

If he wanted to spend any time with Nichole, he'd have to hurry and get through the next two calls on his agenda. "Hey, Richard. Markson here."

"I didn't expect to hear from you today. What's up?"

"I'm ready to upgrade to your Kingston Air X Plus. How long will it take to get it?"

"Wow, I thought you'd never come to your senses. Do you want to trade in your X model?"

"No, that's not going to be possible. I crashed it yesterday." Markson grinned, expecting Richard's reaction.

"What! Are you serious?"

Man, was he predictable? Right on cue, even! "As serious as a heart attack. Thank goodness for the ballistic parachute. I want one on the new jet, as well."

"Dude! Are you in the hospital or something? Why didn't you tell me yesterday?"

"As a matter of fact, I *am* at the hospital, but I'm getting my discharge papers any minute. My passenger and I walked away without a scratch. I'd say the jet could easily be fixed, except it's nearly impossible to recover it from where it landed in the Great Smoky Mountains. We both got injured in the mountains."

"Did your passenger freak out?"

"Aside from ordering another jet, it's my passenger that I wanted to talk to you about. Do you believe in fate?"

"Depends. What are you getting at?"

"Her name is Nichole. I think she's the one."

"The one for what? Markson, did you hit your head in the crash? You're not making much sense."

"It's hard to make any sense when I'm around Nichole. I think she's the one I'm supposed to marry."

"Wow! Are you the same guy who told me that you would never be crazy enough to tie yourself down? She must be amazing for you to change your mind so fast."

How could Markson explain what had happened? He didn't have to. Richard knew all too well since he married Anne-Marie. "There's just one problem."

"What's that?"

"Nichole doesn't know who I am."

"That's pretty big, but I'm sure she'll overlook your billions."

"If only it were that simple. My company basically stole her father's company. She hates everything to do with Rothschild Venture Capital."

"Hmm. That does complicate matters, but it's not insurmountable. You're a resourceful guy. I'm sure you'll figure it out. Let me know if you need any advice; I'm full of it."

"Yeah, you're full of something. Anyway, about the parachute on the new jet."

"Already comes standard. Do you want all of the same interior configurations? Or were you thinking of doing something different?"

"Nothing different. How soon can I get it?"

"I'll put a rush on it. We can have it ready in a month."

"Perfect. Thanks, Richard."

"No problem. I can't wait to tell Anne-Marie your news. She won our bet, you know."

"I don't even want to know. Bye." Markson checked his watch, hating every moment he was apart from Nichole. One more call, then he could go back to her. "Stephen, Markson here."

"Hey, I was just thinking about you. Is everything okay? I had the strangest feeling yesterday that you were in trouble."

"Still haven't lost your touch, I see. I crashed my plane, but that's not why I'm calling."

"Wow, this must be good if the plane crash isn't the headline of this call. What's up?"

"I need your cyber skills to catch a thief. You up for it?"

"Absolutely. Give me what you've got."

"I don't have much to go on right now. His first name is Sal. It sounds like his M.O. is to meet wealthy people at a golf club, become a business partner, sell the company out from under the owner, then take off with the loot. Oh, and there's some petty theft just before he takes it all down. Unfortunately, my intern bought the company, and now I'm trying to see how much hot water I'm going to be in. I'll send you all the deal information to see if you can glean any more information from it."

Stephen softly whistled as he scribbled notes. "This sounds like an interesting challenge. Thanks for letting me work on it. I'll get started right away."

Markson didn't have to worry that Stephen would stick with it until he found every data bit ever recorded about Sal. He was a good friend to have on his side. With everything set in motion, he could spend the next few days concentrating on his newest dream.

CHAPTER 15
NICHOLE

"Well, Dad, what did you think of him?" Nichole would have bounced with excitement on the bed had just the mere idea of it not hurt. She'd never brought a man home before, not like she had much choice with Mark. But her dad's approval meant the world to her. She wondered about the curious expression on her father's face.

"He seems like a nice enough chap. You really like him, don't you?" He scooted the only chair in the cubicle a little closer while he remained seated.

She nodded solemnly while soaking up her father's presence. Never again would she take her time with him for granted. Thinking she might have lost him scared her more than she wanted to admit. It may have only been heartburn, but to her, it was a wake-up call.

"I wonder what Mom would have thought of him. Did she ever talk about who she thought I'd marry, Dad?" She wished she had more memories of her mother, but a six-year-old didn't think about storing mommy-moments. Each year, the few memories she had faded until they almost felt like dreams.

"The only thing she ever said about that was if you found someone as good as myself, then you'd be the happiest woman ever to live." The side of his mouth lifted in a rueful smile.

Nichole knew it hurt her father to speak of her mom. He'd never actually said he didn't want to talk about her, but Nichole felt his sadness whenever she brought up anything to do with her. She could imagine how hard it would be to lose the love of your life to such an insidious and progressive disease as M.S.

The doctor appeared at the curtain entrance, and Nichole's attention immediately reverted to her current situation. With the way her father exhaled and perked up, she could tell he was glad for the interruption.

Mark's face showed through the parted curtains, but he stepped back as soon as he saw the doctor inside. "Mark, it's okay. Come in here. Dr. Benson was just going to go over my condition," Nichole said. She wasn't about to let him leave again. This way, he could hear the doctor's diagnosis, and she wouldn't have to repeat it.

He hesitantly stepped inside, "I didn't want to intrude."

Nichole patted the side of her gurney, hoping Mark would get the hint to come closer. "Not at all. You're right on time." She faced the doctor and said, "What's the verdict?"

"A bad sprain. You'll want to stay off of it as much as possible for the next seven days. Be sure to ice it and take anti-inflammatories as needed. I'm sure you know the drill." Dr. Benson flipped several pages from the lab results before looking over to his patient. "Would you like to see your file?"

"Sure." She took the clipboard. Everything seemed in order, the workup showing just what she expected to see. "Looks like I won't have any problem getting discharged right away then."

"Exactly. You were fortunate this time. Hopefully, I won't see you back here unless it's for you to start working again." He squeezed her toes and smiled. "We are hiring, you know. Anyway, I'll have them get your discharge paperwork ready. It's good seeing you again, Nichole." Dr. Benson nodded to the two men before he turned and left.

Nichole didn't miss the way Mark's eyes narrowed minutely at Dr. Benson when he realized they knew one another. She kept herself from smiling. If he didn't care anything about her, then he wouldn't have reacted that way.

A moment later, a medical assistant entered with her discharge papers. Nichole's fleeting thrill of getting out of there immediately tempered with the idea that Mark would leave. How was she supposed to discover what could happen between them if he weren't around? Yet, she couldn't see any way around her problem. Nichole signed her name and handed the papers back to the woman.

"It looks like your bill has already been paid, so you're all set to go," the young lady announced. "I'll bring the wheelchair, and we can get you to your car."

"What's this? How?" Nichole turned an accusing eye toward her dad.

He held up his hand defensively. "Don't look at me. I'm just as surprised as you are."

As one, Nichole and Jacob turned to look at Mark. "Guilty. My company paid for everything. Decreases any liability."

"That's ridiculous, Mark. I'll pay them back. I have insurance, you know."

"Don't bother. It's already done. Don't think another thing about it. I'm glad you're getting sprung, Nichole. I guess I'll get out of your hair and head over to my hotel. It was nice meeting you, Jacob."

Jacob stood, his body straight and his tone firm. "Now, wait just a minute, Mark. There's no way you're going to be staying in a hotel. You'll come and stay with us. We have plenty of room. I won't take no for an answer."

Had she been standing, Nichole would have hugged her father. As it was, she grinned as she looked back and forth between her dad and Mark. This battle of wills amused her, and she desperately hoped her dad won.

"I don't want to intrude. I mean, Nichole might not want me—"

Nichole grinned. "I learned a long time ago not to argue with him. You'd be wise just to concede right now and save yourself the trouble."

MARKSON

Since he didn't have a hotel to go to anyway, this couldn't have worked out any better. Plus, not enough time had passed for Brittney to purchase a house for him. She was good at her job, but nobody could pull that off in only a couple of hours.

With Jacob's blessing, he could visit with both Nichole and Jacob without it seeming contrived or strange. More than pleased, he smiled. "Thank you. I accept your generous offer.

If I can get your address, then I'll come over as soon as I get a car rented."

"Nonsense, Mark. You can ride home with us. I insist." Jacob nodded as if this conversation were over.

Looking down at Nichole, he said, "I see where you get your stubborn streak." No longer did she have worry lines etched across her forehead or beside her mouth.

She looked younger and more vibrant than he'd ever seen her. A sparkle showed in her eyes, possibly because she was getting to spend more time with him. He hoped that was the reason. His ego wanted to believe that was true.

Another nurse brought a wheelchair. Markson didn't wait for anyone to interfere but took matters into his hands. Literally. He plucked Nichole from the bed and gently placed her in the wheelchair.

"Sorry, it was too painful to watch you struggle into the bed." That was the only apology she was going to get from him. Not that he had any regrets; he'd do it again in a heartbeat. In fact, he'd probably carry her into her father's house if she'd let him.

The ride to their house was generally quiet. Markson split his time between texting his plans to Brittney and watching the scenery. As he'd never been to this part of Tennessee before, he enjoyed seeing the beautiful little town. Their house was in a very nice neighborhood, which shouldn't have surprised him.

As they drove, he sent a text to Brittney asking her to arrange for a private chef. The Monroe family might be offering him a room, but he'd supply the meals for compensation. Plus, he didn't want Nichole or Jacob to worry about preparing meals for him.

He paid particular attention to the houses, trying to decide which one Brittney would buy. He didn't see any sale signs in the yards, but that didn't mean they couldn't be purchased—enough money could buy almost anything. No matter which house she bought, they were all relatively new and quite lovely by the town's standards.

They turned down another street where Markson saw a moving van parked in a driveway. Was that there because of him? It seemed very likely—even more likely when they parked in a driveway only three houses away.

"Home, sweet home," Nichole said.

"It's very nice. How long have you lived here?" Markson let himself out of the SUV and hurried to the passenger door to help Nichole.

Jacob monitored their progress and said, "I bought this place about eight years ago. It's a bit big, especially when Nichole's away on a job assignment, but I liked it the moment I laid my eyes on it."

Nichole craned her neck to see around Markson's shoulder. "Dad, it looks like the Smythe's are moving out."

Jacob didn't bother looking as he gathered a few items from the truck. "Good riddance. They were trying to get restrictions added to our properties. Nobody was pleased with his petition."

Nichole made a strange noise before she dismissively shook her head. "Seems odd that they'd suddenly decide to move. I guess they got the message loud and clear."

Markson's lips twitched, but he managed to keep his composure. He doubly hoped Brittney had bought that house, especially if it solved a neighborhood problem. His arm around Nichole's waist took more of her weight as they made slow, limping progress toward the front door.

Even though it would have been easier to carry her, she didn't want to make a spectacle in their neighborhood. He understood, but it still irked him that he couldn't just take charge in spite of their neighbors. For now, he'd follow her lead.

They hadn't even been inside the house for more than twenty minutes before the doorbell rang. Jacob went to answer it, leaving Markson and Nichole alone in the living room. "I really don't mind staying in a hotel, Nichole. It was nice of your dad to offer to let me stay, but I don't want to intrude."

"Can I be honest?" Nichole looked anywhere but at Markson.

What if she told him to leave? He'd honor her wishes, of course, but it would be a crushing blow to his ego. His throat went dry, but he managed to sound halfway normal as he answered her. "Certainly. I'd expect nothing less."

"I wanted you to stay."

His heart did silly flip-flops in his chest. He hadn't felt like this since Amber told him she'd go to the winter dance with him in junior high school. "You did?" A grin released the tension he had been holding inside.

He would have loved to continue with this conversation, but Jacob's discussion with whoever knocked on the door came through loud and clear. "I'm telling you, you have the wrong house. I didn't arrange for a personal chef."

Nichole's eyes darted over to Markson's, and she frowned. "Oops. I better go take care of that." Markson jumped from the couch and raced out of the room. He had to straighten out this situation before it got out of hand. "Jacob, I'm sorry. I lost track of time."

Shifting his gaze from his host to his guest, Markson said, "You must be Emmit."

"Yes." He sighed, his relief evident.

"Jacob, this is Emmit. My work arranged for him to make meals for all of us as long as I stay here. I hope you don't mind, but I didn't want to put you out in any way. It's the least I can do to repay your generosity in allowing me to stay here. Please say you'll accept this payment."

Instantly, Jacob nodded. "Oh, well, certainly. You would have figured out pretty quick that I'm a terrible cook."

"I can attest to that!" Nichole yelled from the living room.

Laughter followed as Emmit entered the house, following Jacob into the kitchen. Markson tried to stay with them, but Jacob waved him away to go back to Nichole.

"What's going on?" Nichole asked before Markson even resumed his seat.

"Prepared meals are a perk from my job. The office arranged for the chef to come here." He wished he would have said something before the man showed up.

"How did they know where to send him?" The way Nichole's eyes narrowed suspiciously told Markson to tread lightly.

"I texted them the address. I hope you're hungry." With the way Nichole perked up, he knew he'd struck the right chord.

"I'm so hungry; I could eat a cow!"

He hadn't expected that answer and began chuckling. "That's a relief because we're having Japanese Wagyu beef boneless ribeye steak."

"You know, your job sounds pretty swanky. First, they give you that Rolex, and now you're telling me you get some of the most expensive steaks in the world as a perk. I need to get a new career. Maybe I'll come work with you."

Even though he knew she was joking, it both thrilled and scared Markson to envision it. He had to steer this conversation to safer ground, or she might kick him out before the meat made it into the oven. "Dinner's going to be in about thirty minutes. Did you want to take a shower first?"

"That sounds heavenly. I'm ready to get out of this outfit and into something comfier." She struggled to her feet, waving off his assistance. "I can't have you moving me around like I'm an invalid. Besides, a little movement will keep it from getting too stiff."

Markson watched her go, wishing he could stay glued to her side. He certainly wouldn't mind the assignment. A few minutes later, Jacob came to the doorway, looking around with a confused expression. "Where's Nichole?"

"Shower." Markson stood. "I'd like to talk to you about Sal while we have a moment to ourselves. Do you mind?"

"Sure. Come into my office."

Markson hadn't expected the office to be quite so fine with the built-in mahogany bookcases on two walls and the oversized desk in the middle of the room. Jacob's business had been prosperous enough to finance this home, and he held that company in his portfolio. He'd have to ask Brittney about any outstanding mortgage Jacob might have on the house. The last thing he wanted was to be the cause for Nichole's father losing his home.

He sat in the plush leather chair across from Jacob, propping his ankle on his knee. "I spoke with my friend, Stephen. He was eager to get started on tracking down Sal. He geeks out on puzzles like yours."

"Sounds like a good friend to have in your corner." Jacob nodded appreciatively.

"Definitely. He needs as much information about Sal as you can give him. His last name would be a great help, employment records, resume, birthday, favorite hangouts, family—pretty much anything you can remember about him. From what Nichole told me, it sounds like you might not be the first person Sal did this to. It would be nice to get him stopped."

"I never thought about that. You're right. How soon do you need the information?" Jacob drummed his fingers on his thigh with one hand while his other hand pressed against his cheek.

"The sooner, the better."

"I'll work on it tonight. I'll email you what I come up with. What's your email address?"

Markson spotted a notepad on the desk. Reaching over, he asked, "Mind if I write it down for you?"

"Go ahead."

No sooner had he finished and set it back on the desk, than Nichole appeared in the doorway. "What's going on in here? How come I keep finding the two of you with your heads together?"

Jacob laughed, and Markson's mouth opened and closed as he tried to come up with something intelligent to say.

Emmit appeared next to Nichole. "Dinner's ready."

Markson would have cried out in relief, but he had to restrain himself. Thank goodness for perfect timing. "Thanks, Emmit. It smells amazing."

CHAPTER 16

NICHOLE

Nichole opened her eyes to see the muted decorations of her bedroom. Of course, it had all been a dream. She should have known that reality couldn't possibly offer her something so perfect. Hugging her pillow to her chest, she clenched her eyes shut, willing herself to fall back asleep to let it continue for just a bit longer.

The movement onto her side tweaked her knee, radiating sharp pain all across it. Had it been a dream? If so, why would her knee be injured? Hope blossomed again; she'd gladly take the pain if it meant she could also have more time with Mark.

The sound of her father whistling in his office filtered down to her bedroom. She loved hearing his joyful noise, reminding her once again that she came home for his health scare. That concern turned out to be unfounded.

Now, if only Mark had indeed come to stay with them, then she could rejoice in waking. The other two pieces of evidence proved this to be her reality; then, it seemed evident that Mark had spent the night.

Carefully rolling onto her back, she stared up toward her ceiling yet not seeing anything in her room. Snippets of memories of her time with Mark flashed across her thoughts. How could she feel so close to him in such a short amount of time? Were her feelings real, or were they only a manifestation of her gratefulness for surviving their near-death experience together?

She might have been able to convince herself of this except for the kiss they'd shared. The sparks between them had been real, intense, and unexpected. And, Mark had promised to stay by her side until she told him to leave, that had to say something about how he felt.

She would have imagined herself to be much clearer on how to tell if a guy liked her, especially at her age. "Mom, I sure wish you were around," she whispered. Nichole had lost track of how many times she'd said that phrase throughout her life.

Yet, thinking about her mom tempered her excitement about falling for Mark. What if he wanted to have kids? She couldn't give him any. It wouldn't be fair to snare him into a relationship without full disclosure.

How would she bring that up in a casual conversation? "Oh, my mom died from complications of M.S. Any children I'd have could contract the debilitating disease, and I won't take the chance. Hope that doesn't bother you."

No matter how many times she replayed the scenario in her head, it always sounded stilted and selfish. She'd never had to worry about any of this with Jaxson. He didn't want kids. He made that abundantly clear from day one, which bothered her then.

How long would she let her memories of Jaxson hijack her from moving forward? He'd done quite the number on her self-esteem. She didn't notice it so much anymore when she buried herself in her work, but she couldn't ignore it forever.

Grabbing the notebook and pen from her nightstand, she tore out a blank page from the back of the book. Even though this seemed like a pointless gesture, she made herself go through the motions.

She began writing her goodbye letter to Jaxson. "Jaxson, you've stolen too much of my life with your selfish ways. I no longer accept the things you said to me and about me to others. None of those things are true.

"From this point on, you are nothing to me. You no longer have any say in who I see or what I say. I don't have to prove anything to you, nor do I have to behave in a certain way to be acceptable to my friends. I don't have to be an athlete. I help people in ways you never will.

"I am good enough. I am smart enough. I am beautiful.

"Goodbye, Jaxson. I hope you find happiness in your heart and your life. I hope you find a woman you will adore, someone who makes you want to be a better person."

She didn't sign her name. Instead, she drew a smiley face. Yes, that seemed more appropriate for how she felt. After reading through it two more times, she nodded her agreement.

With halting, painful steps, she crossed her room to get to her bathroom. Standing over the toilet, she ripped the note into tiny shreds and let them flutter down into the privy. Tears blurred her eyes, and one dropped into the water as she leaned forward to press the lever. The pent-up hurt swirled through her mind at the same rate as the water inside the porcelain bowl. The water gurgled and disappeared forever. "Goodbye, Jaxson," she whispered.

One of the patients she'd worked with told me how she'd done this after a breakup. At the time, she'd thought it mostly a silly gesture, but now she felt the release. It might be symbolic or even a placebo, but it did shift something inside her. She was ready to move on. Hopefully, Mark wanted the same thing.

Even with her slow progress, she felt lighter on her feet. The morning shower had cleared out the last of her sleepiness. Now, a cup of coffee would improve her outlook on recovery.

She entered the kitchen and stopped cold. Never before had she seen so much food in her father's house. This veritable buffet of delicious-looking breakfast food had to be Mark's handiwork.

The man in question entered the room with her father. "Dad, please tell me you've finally learned how to cook." She grinned, knowing he'd have to deny it. He was quite possibly the worst cook in the whole world. From the age of six, she'd learned to fend for herself in the food department.

"Sorry, cutie. Emmit left a couple of minutes ago. I was just getting ready to wake you up when I heard your shower going. Did you sleep well?" Jacob leaned over and kissed Nichole's cheek before he grabbed a plate to start dishing his breakfast.

"I slept like a ton. Those pain pills must have helped." She grabbed a plate then looked over to Mark. Heat rushed through her at seeing him in her house. His damp hair still sparkled from his shower, and his easy smile made her stomach do flip-flops. "How was your night, Mark?"

"Wonderful. At least I didn't have to worry about a wild creature attacking me while I slept."

Nichole laughed. "From how loudly you were snoring in the forest, it's a wonder anything came anywhere near our campsite."

Mark shook his head. "My snoring? You should have heard yours."

"Okay, children. It's time to eat." Jacob grabbed his silverware and stepped over to the table.

Nichole leaned close to Mark and whispered, "I don't snore."

"Ha! I'll record it next time. Hey, are you going to dish your food or wait for it to all go cold?" He reached across her to ladle some scrambled eggs.

The white from his bandage caught her eye. How could she have forgotten about his injury? What kind of nurse was she to be so forgetful and thoughtless? She'd blame it on her medication, but it still irked her. "How does your hand feel today?"

"Changing the subject, I see. It's fine. It only hurts when I use it or move it. I should be good to go in about a week. Hopefully, this food will help with my nausea. Those antibiotics will be the death of me."

"It should help." She glanced at his stomach, only then realizing his outfit. "Where'd you get those clothes? They don't look like anything my father owns."

"A courier brought them first thing this morning." Mark kept his focus solely on the plate he piled high with food.

Nichole frowned. "Let me guess, another job perk?"

"Yep. Who knew all I had to do was crash the company jet to get a whole new wardrobe?"

It took Nichole a second to process what he said. Her eyes flew up to his face, and seeing his serious expression shocked her. "I sure hope you're kidding."

Mark chuckled and left her to sit beside Jacob. "It's way too easy to tease you."

She couldn't believe she fell for his jesting yet again. Hobbling slowly, she set her plate down and pressed her hands against the side of the table to ease herself into the chair. Her fork only made it halfway to her mouth before she looked at her father's nearly empty plate. "Are you in a hurry, Dad?"

"Yep. George reserved us an eight o'clock tee time. I'd invite you and Mark, but I don't think either of you is physically up to the game. Besides, you don't need me hanging around here, hovering and getting in the way." His chair's legs scraped loudly across the planks of the floor as he stood. "I won't be home until this evening. Have fun, kids."

Nichole's fork remained frozen as she saw her dad practically running to get out of the house. She'd never before seen him so eager to go golfing. Now, what was he up to? The garage door opened and closed before Nichole blinked and felt like she came out of a trance. "Do you believe him?" She turned to Mark.

He lifted one shoulder, apparently unphased by how quickly they'd been left alone. "He loves his golf. I dare say I'm glad I wasn't able to go with him. I'm astonishingly bad at it."

She ate in silence, her mind whirling with what to do with this newfound alone time with Mark. Scraping the last bite onto her fork, she said, "I think we need to talk."

"That sounds ominous. What's up?" Mark stood, holding his plate in his hand. He raised an eyebrow toward her, where his hand hovered next to hers.

"I'm done. Thank you." The clanking of her fork against the plate set her nerves on edge. It was strange, but a pleasant change, to have someone else take charge of the cleanup. Yet the play of his muscles underneath the tight teeshirt only intensified her troubled thoughts. If this conversation didn't go as she planned, she shouldn't get too used to it all.

"Why don't you head into the living room, and I'll meet you there in a minute." The water splashed over the plates noisily. He glanced over his shoulder and added, "Unless you want me to carry you."

Yes! Her heart screamed to accept his playful offer. She would love to be pressed against his hard chest. It would be amazing to breathe in his masculine scent. But her mind adamantly refused. "No, I need to have some activity, or my whole body won't work right."

"It's your loss."

"You got that right," she mumbled when she hobbled into the living room. She never noticed the vast distance between the couch and the kitchen. Nor had she realized how hard it was to lift her leg onto the cushion without using her knee or bending it.

Mark's hand dropped to grasp her heel, gently cradling it until she spun herself around to lay it flat. "Thanks."

Instead of moving across from her, Mark sat next to her foot with his fingers resting over her toes. His actions were making her more nervous about speaking what needed to be said.

"So, what's going on? You sounded so serious in the kitchen. If you're having second thoughts about me staying here, I can—."

"No, it's not as simple as that." How was she supposed to say what was on her heart without getting her heart broken if he didn't share her feelings?

"Honestly, Nichole, I don't want to make you uncomfortable. Something is bothering you." He removed his hand, leaving a cold spot behind.

Her vision focused on his hand, willing it to touch her again. Was she right to open this conversation up, or should she let the week go by with it left unsaid? Once he had his follow-up appointment with the hospital, he'd return to Atlanta. How long would she regret her silence? She had to speak now or forever hold her peace.

"You're right. Something is bothering me, but it's not because of you. Well, it is because of you. Well. Okay, this isn't coming out the way I planned."

"It's okay. Take a deep breath and start over. I don't have anywhere to be. We've got plenty of time."

She loved seeing his smile, wishing it could be hers to have for the rest of her life. But, he'd said one key phrase that hit home. They didn't have plenty of time, and he did have somewhere else to be. Atlanta. And her life was here in Gatlinburg. How could she ask him to leave his home town? Would he even want to?

Inhaling didn't give her any additional clarity for this strange situation, but it did buy her some time. Mark's look of concern wasn't helping. Time to rip off the bandage.

"Okay, Mark. We're both adults here. I'm just going to lay my cards on the table, and then we can go from there." It felt good to lay the foundation for how this discussion would go.

"Sounds reasonable."

He crossed his arms, letting Nichole see the muscles flex. If only he wouldn't be so distracting, she'd have an easier time of this. "So, I like you, Mark."

"I like you, too."

She did her best to ignore him and his almost-grin. He was playing with her, and she wasn't going to take the bait this time. "It's crazy because we've only known each other for a day, but I feel as though I've known you for a lifetime."

"That sounds like a good thing."

"You know, this would be a lot easier if you'd stop interrupting me."

She rolled her eyes when he mimed zipping his lips shut. She'd have to take advantage of this moment's reprieve. "Mark, I've never felt for anyone the way I feel for you. Frankly, it scares me more than a little bit. I halfway expect you to run out of the house screaming." Exhaling, she added, "I love you, Mark.

Mark's eyes widened, and he shook his head. "I can't believe you just said that."

Nichole knew she should have kept that to herself. This was precisely the reaction she'd been avoiding. "Mark, I—," she didn't get any further because his phone rang. She hoped he'd ignore it, but a part of her welcomed the distraction.

He pulled the phone from his pocket. "Sorry, I've got to take this."

It looked as though he couldn't get away fast enough. She couldn't blame him. He left the room, leaving her to cry alone without making him pity her on top of everything else.

CHAPTER 17

MARKSON

The timing couldn't have been any worse, but he had to take the call. He hurried out the back door and swiped the screen to answer. "Hey, Brittney."

"Hi, Markson. Sorry to bother you, but I have good news."

"Great. What is it?" He pinched the bridge of his nose, wishing he could get this over with and get back to Nichole. He hated seeing her struggle to share her feelings with him, only to have him leave at her most vulnerable moment.

"The house sale finalized, and the keys will be delivered by courier tomorrow along with the SUV you requested. Both are in Nichole Childress's name."

"Wonderful. Who were the previous owners?" Even though he didn't have time for this, his curiosity was piqued. He heard paperwork crinkling as he assumed Brittney searched.

"Hmm, let's see. It looks like Ezekiel and Cali Smythe. Do you want the address now? All of the paperwork will be delivered with the keys."

"No, that's fine. I can wait." He'd been right about the house. The neighborhood would be happier with the Smythe's gone. He glanced at his watch, impatient to return to Nichole.

"Okay. We've scheduled a team to come out and furnish it today. Do you have any preferences?"

Markson didn't care what it looked like, but he had to consider what Nichole would want. Bearing in mind the style of Jacob's house, he said, "Maybe modern country. Nothing retro or too modern. This isn't my forte, and I hope I'm making sense. I'll take a few pictures inside Jacob's house, and you can go from there."

"Perfect. Okay, next up. Legal has finished looking over the documents you requested, and they have come up with a plan to rescind the contract. They should have everything handled by next week. Did you have anything new you wanted me to work on?"

"I was thinking about a piece of jewelry. Something nice from Aurora-Baton's. I'll text you the details later tonight.

Also, I'd like a couple of my dark suits delivered. I have a few plans of my own."

"Sounds interesting. I can't wait to hear all about it. Have a nice day, Markson."

Markson smiled down at the phone, glad to have such an efficient assistant who didn't feel the need to make idle conversation. He snapped a few photos and texted them directly to Brittney on his way back to the living room. With that done, he could focus entirely on Nichole.

First thing, he had to fix the angst he'd caused by his abrupt departure. He had the perfect method in mind. Turning from the hallway, he stopped short when he saw the empty couch. Where did she go?

A sniffling noise caught his attention, and he turned toward the floor-to-ceiling windows. Nichole stood silhouetted by the bright morning sunshine, creating a halo that made him realize she was his angel. And he'd hurt her. He felt as bad as a little boy who accidentally broke a bird's wing.

He couldn't let this go on. This untenable situation required him to take action. Calling out softly, he said, "Nichole?" Her shoulders stiffened, and her hand hastily rose to her cheek. She needed a moment to compose herself.

On his way across the room, he grabbed a couple of tissues from the box. Staying behind her, he held out them out like some lame peace offering. The next time he gave her something, it would make her feel like the queen she already was. He patiently waited while she blew her nose and wiped her eyes. As soon as she seemed composed, he put his hands on her shoulders and forced her to turn to face him.

Her eyes were red and puffy. He'd caused this. "I'm sorry, Nichole." Gently rubbing his thumb across her cheek, he wiped away a tear she'd missed. "I want to clarify something with you. Sometimes words don't work well for me."

Rather than bungle up this situation any further, he leaned in until his lips touched hers. He put his arms around her back and stepped closer so she wouldn't have to move. In case she wanted to escape, he didn't press the kiss but let her take the lead. When she moaned softly, his heart jittered against his ribs.

Pulling away, he rested his forehead against hers. "I can't believe this."

He felt her body stiffen against his. "What's wrong?"

"Nothing is wrong. You're perfect, Nichole. Impossibly perfect. I can't believe I'm so lucky to have found you. When you said you loved me, I wanted to shout with joy.

"I didn't know if you felt the same for me as I did for you. You're far braver than I am, Nichole. I didn't want to scare you away by declaring my love for you. But you said it first."

"So, it's true? You love me?" Nichole bit her bottom lip, uncertainty plain for anyone to see. Her eyes pleaded with him to accept her.

How could she still question how he felt? He'd fix that right now and make it impossible for her to misconstrue his intentions. "Yes. I love you, Nichole. I don't know how or why, but God has brought us together under impossible circumstances. I hope I'll be worthy of your love, and I promise to try to make each and every day of your life better than the last."

Another tear dripped down her cheek, but her smile almost overwhelmed his heart. Seeing her so happy transformed her from beautiful to angelic. And she wanted him. He couldn't believe his luck.

"But you live in Atlanta. How's that supposed to work?"

He chuckled. "Are you trying to find an excuse to get out of this?"

"No! I just—I just don't want to leave my father. With everything he's been going through, it's made me realize that he needs me. I've been selfish with my career and my time, but I can't do that to him anymore." She winced as her body shifted.

"Let's talk about this on the couch. You've been on your feet too long." He gently scooped her up in his arms, loving how she melted against him like a second skin. Rather than let her go, he sat down and kept her in his lap. This is how they were always meant to be. "Is this okay?"

"Perfect. But, Mark, there's something I need to tell you before we let things go any farther."

"There's nothing we can't handle together."

She leaned away slightly, her hand resting on his chest. "We can't ever have children together."

He hadn't expected that. She looked healthy. Did she not like kids? "Why?"

She exhaled slowly, composing herself to answer. "My mom died of MS. That makes me a carrier, and I wouldn't want to watch a child of mine go through such a horrible death. We could adopt or get a surrogate. But I just can't. I hope you can understand."

"I do understand. Have you ever been tested to see if you're a carrier? Medical research has come a long way in genetic coding."

"It's expensive, and I've never needed to know for sure. I've lived with the possibility for so long that I convinced myself that it was out of the question."

"I don't care about the cost. It's nothing compared to the value of knowing the truth. Tell me, if you knew you didn't have the gene, would you want to have children?"

"Absolutely. I'd have as many as the good Lord wanted me to have. Children are such a blessing. How about you? Do you want kids? Some men don't, but we should agree on this if we plan to see what is happening between us. Right?"

"To be honest, I never thought I'd get married, let alone have kids. But, I like the idea. Especially with you. Can you imagine six little girls with your eyes running around? Yes, I'd like that very much." He stared into her eyes, willing her to see past his humor to his sincerity.

"What was your childhood like?"

Nichole's question came so unexpectedly; his mind went totally blank. How could he explain growing up with unimaginable wealth? Now would be a good time to tell her the truth, but their relationship was too fresh and fragile to tarnish.

"I'd say I had a pretty typical childhood. My parents were very devoted and loving. I remember my dad would come home from work and always have time for me." He laughed at the memory of himself.

"It makes me feel guilty now. I never realized how many hours each day he put into his job, but when he got home, I'd go racing outside to be the first one to welcome him home. He'd have a massive smile on his face as he got out of the car.

"He'd kneel on the ground, arms outstretched to hug me when I flew into him. He'd jump up and throw me in the air and catch me. Every single day, rain or shine. Then he'd ask me if I'd been a good boy."

Nichole tucked herself against his shoulder. She hummed with pleasure, "I can totally see that. I bet you were an adorable little boy."

He growled. "I hope I still am."

"Oh, no. We've already established that you're gorgeous now." She tweaked the muscles on his arm and said, "Way too muscular for mere cute."

"Well, it's official. I'm keeping you around if only to stroke my ego if I ever get down."

"Somehow, I doubt you need much of that."

If she only knew. He inhaled, loving the strawberry shampoo she used. He'd never think of strawberries the same again. "Hey, do you have any allergies? Or are there some foods you refuse to eat? Emmit is planning the menu for the week and wanted to know. I already know you like foreign foods like crickets, which Emmit said he had a great recipe, by the way. But is there anything else?"

"You did not! What gave you that impression" She pushed herself up until she could look him in the eyes.

"Of course. You told me yourself. Remember? When we were beside the campfire, you said we could eat the crickets. Lots of protein. I know that's what you said, so don't try to deny it. Emmit has the perfect recipe for tonight's dinner. You're going to love it."

She slapped his chest. "Stop it. You better be kidding, or you'll be eating alone. I refuse to eat any kind of bug or creepy-crawly, including escargot. I won't eat something that leaves a slime trail behind itself."

"I love it when you get riled. Your eyes light up beautifully. Let me see them closer." He pulled her against him, his lips finding hers.

His plan backfired when her lashes fluttered closed. He followed suit, and he let his other senses take over, feeling his love pour into her through their passionate kiss. Time could freeze on this moment, and he'd be the happiest man who ever lived.

Throughout the day, he'd looked forward to this moment. "I hope you like fondu. There's a cheese one for dinner and a chocolate one for dessert. I thought we could sit by the fire and relax." Markson carried the last platter containing fruit for the chocolate. He could already envision himself feeding Nichole and watching her enjoy it.

Never before had he known the pleasure of sharing food. The women he'd dated had all eaten like birds or rabbits. He loved how Nichole enjoyed a steak or a dessert with as much relish as he did. The more time they spent together, the harder it would be if she tired of him.

He'd wanted to set up a blanket and pillows on the floor, but Nichole's knee injury made that impractical. Instead, he'd shifted the couch, so it faced the fire, but far enough away for them to enjoy the ambiance without roasting. He'd adjusted the gas, so the flames were low and welcoming.

"Emmit didn't include a pot of crickets for dipping, did he?" She asked as she hobbled slowly across the room.

"I'm pretty sure I heard that anything dipped in chocolate is amazing. Are you saying that might not be true?" He stepped over to help Nichole ease herself onto the couch.

Adjusting a pillow to brace her knee, he pulled the food tray closer.

"I'm saying I don't want to find out. No bugs. That's my rule." She craned her neck to investigate the buffet before looking around with her eyebrows drawn down. "Where's dad?"

"He's having Wagyu steak and lobster in the kitchen."

"Why isn't he eating with us?"

"He said he wanted to get some work done and didn't want to disturb us. Between you and me, I think he just wanted to find out Emmit's secret seasoning for the steak." He didn't want to mention that Jacob had said three was a crowd. Tonight, he was inclined to agree with him.

Nichole chuckled. "I honestly don't think it'll help Dad's cooking." The happy lines of her mouth flattened. "I don't know where your company found Emmit, but I'm going to miss this when you're gone."

Markson turned and stared at her, blinking several times. "Who said I was going anywhere?"

"We both know, you and I have to work. It's not like we can turn off our lives just because we found love. If that were the case for lovebirds, then a lot of people would be homeless and starving.

He didn't want to think about leaving or work. The only thing he wanted to concentrate on was making Nichole happy. He'd made a promise, if only to himself. Nichole was his priority; everything else came a distant second.

CHAPTER 18

MARKSON

"I sent you the report. Did you get it yet?" Stephen asked.

Markson swiped open the message on his phone and downloaded the file. After only a minute to read it, he softly whistled. "It looks like Sal's been a naughty boy. How did you manage to put all this together so fast?" And why wasn't he already in jail? Sal's exploits extended much farther than Markson had initially believed with several pages of alleged crimes he'd perpetrated.

"Fast—are you kidding? It took me almost a whole week, and I started to think I was losing my edge. Although, once you gave me the information Jacob put together, it was a simple matter of inputting the data points and locating the intersections—."

"Okay, okay. I'm sorry I asked. Jeez, Stephen, don't give away all of your trade secrets. Plus, your data-mining genius is completely wasted on someone like me." Markson had long since learned that it was nearly impossible to get a word in edgewise once he got Stephen started.

Nichole hadn't stirred from her bedroom yet. If he hurried, he could share this with Jacob without her being any the wiser. "Thanks for everything, Stephen. Have you sent this report to the authorities yet?"

"Yep, just before I called you. I'm pretty sure the local police will have him picked up within the next ten minutes. He just charged a drink at the casino and sat down to play another round of Blackjack. Luckily, the Vegas casinos have excellent surveillance footage to keep track of his movements."

Relief washed through him over Stephen's initiative. If they left the matter up to Jacob, no charges would ever be filed against Sal. Markson couldn't understand Jacob's attitude unless he was embarrassed to get duped by Sal. He could relate to that feeling. Nobody liked being made to look like a fool.

Markson glanced at his Rolex. Either Sal hadn't gone to bed yet, or he didn't worry about how early he started drinking. He almost wished he could watch the con-artist get arrested. Whose money was he using to fuel his gambling habit? "What happened with the money he stole from Jacob?"

"I already transferred it from Sal's offshore bank account into one in Jacob's name. He can access it whenever he likes. The login information is included in my report, page six, I believe.

"I'll say one thing for Sal; he kept meticulous records of his thefts. He had a separate bank account for each of his heists. It was a cinch to tell which one belonged to Jacob."

That news came as a relief. Although, Markson would have made it right by Jacob, no matter what Stephen had found. "Good work, Stephen. I owe you one."

"Think nothing of it. You know I loved every minute of it. Sometimes, it's nice to research something other than IPOs and cryptocurrencies. Speaking of which, I have an IPO that's opening today."

"I'll let you get back to it then." Markson followed the sound of Jacob's whistle to find him in his office. After a quick tap on the door to catch his attention, he said, "Do you have a minute?"

"Sure, Mark. Come sit down. What's on your mind, son?"

"Do you mind if I airdrop a document to your printer? There's something you need to see."

He gestured toward the device and said, "Be my guest. I'm assuming it's about Sal."

"You bet, and I think you're going to be amazed at what Stephen found out about him. He's quite the piece of work."

"Stephen or Sal?"

"Both really, but for dynamically opposed reasons. One uses his powers for good, and the other is definitely for evil. You'll see." As each page finished printing, he handed it to Jacob. Once he finished reading the whole report, Markson said, "You had no way of knowing Sal could be so crooked. Stephen already sent this to the authorities, and Sal is probably already in custody. The question I have now is whether or not you want to file charges against him. I can't tell you what to do, but the only way to stop people like him is to stand up to him and put him behind bars."

"You're right." Jacob pinched the bridge of his nose, and he heavily sighed. "I just don't have any idea where to start. I'm tired of all of it, Mark."

"Don't worry about it, Jacob. I'll take care of everything."

"You really don't have to."

"We've been down this road before, Jacob. I offered."

"Well, thank you. If there's anything I can ever do to repay you, just let me know."

Markson leaned back in the chair, his fingers rubbing his chin as he thought about his next move. "Well, there is something."

"Name it."

"It's about Nichole." Another round of nerves struck him hard. He rubbed his suddenly damp and trembling hands down the thighs of his jeans.

"Ah!" Jacob leaned forward with his hands folded on top of the desk. "What did you have in mind?"

How could he explain how he truly felt to Nichole's father? He didn't want to come off as arrogant or flippant, but he had to sound confident. No father wanted a spineless wimp for his daughter.

"I'd like to have your permission to ask her to marry me. I hope you can see I have the means to provide for her, and I love her." Once she knew the depth of his feelings for her, then he could reveal the truth of his identity. Until then, he would know that she loved him for himself and not his money. Not that he ever believed Nichole could be motivated by wealth; that just wasn't part of her makeup.

"I can see how much you love her." Jacob nodded his agreement. "And your job does give you nice perks."

Markson's eyebrow rose. "You don't even know the half of it. I can do so much more." And he would. He'd make sure she had everything she ever wanted, including his undying love and devotion.

Jacob nodded again, his piercing gaze bored into Markson. "Where would you live? I know Nichole said she wants to stay with me, but I don't think that's in her best interest. I didn't raise her to be my caretaker. She has to live her own life. I know she loves the countryside here in Gatlinburg, but she thrives when she's helping people."

Markson nodded with each of Jacob's statements. Thankfully, he was in complete agreement, and Markson had a solution. "I thought maybe we could have a house nearby so we could come and visit, but we'd live and work in Atlanta. With my company's private jet, we could visit whenever she'd like."

"Hopefully, the next flight will be less eventful."

Jacob's deadpan statement caught Markson off-guard. Yet, something about Jacob's fleeting expression made him wonder. "We ordered the next generation of that jet, which also includes the ballistic parachute. Anymore, I won't fly without that extra measure of protection. But, if you prefer, we can drive."

"Nah, I'm just messing with you. I know flying is safer than driving. You can do whichever makes you happier."

Markson couldn't agree more about the safety factor. "As for her work, she could continue to be an itinerant nurse, or my company has a project management position open. I think she'd be amazing at it. There's even a humanitarian project that specializes in bringing healthcare to underserved communities."

"It sounds like you've put a lot of thought into what would make Nichole the happiest. I'm glad; that gives me peace of mind."

"Yes. She occupies my every thought. I'd do anything for her. Now, about my question. Do you need more time?"

"No. Mark, over the past week, I've seen how you are with Nichole. More importantly, I've seen how happy Nichole has been since you've stayed here with us. I'd be pleased to call you my son. You have my permission to ask Nichole to marry you."

Relief rushed through Markson. He stood and held out his hand across the desk. Luckily, the antibiotics had taken care of his infection. The bandage across his palm no longer made using his hand a chore. Not that he would have cared at this moment.

Jacob took his hand in a firm grip, which he returned. He knew his broad grin matched Jacob's. This agreement was probably the most important deal he'd ever struck. Now, he just had to get Nichole to agree to his terms, or it would all fall apart.

NICHOLE

The house was strangely quiet. Usually, she'd wake to her father's whistles. She didn't think he had a golf game scheduled. Curiosity had her rushing through her morning routine. As soon as she left her bedroom, she heard muted voices coming from her father's office. Did they have a visitor?

"What are you two up to now?" Nichole asked from the doorway.

Both men snatched their hands away. Their guilty expressions should have caused Nichole more alarm, but she had to laugh. "You two look like you've been caught with your hand in the cookie jar. What's going on?"

Mark spoke up first. "Nothing much. I was just telling your father about a project my friend is working on."

That didn't fly with her. "Really? A project that required the two of you to shake hands on it, huh?"

Mark shrugged. "It's a guy thing. Hey, I thought we could sit out back on the porch. It's turning into a nice day with the sun shining."

"Sure, but we won't have much time. I have my follow-up appointment with Dr. Benson this morning." She had to hide her grin after seeing Mark's immediate reaction.

"I'll drive you. Maybe I'll have him check my hand, too."

She didn't believe his lame excuse for tagging along. Anyone with eyes could see that Mark was jealous of Dr. Benson. But, she'd play along anyway. "Any excuse to drive that fancy new SUV your company loaned you, huh?"

"You bet. If the doctor gives you the all-clear, I might even let you drive us home. How does that sound?"

"Let me, huh? I'm not sure I like that at all."

"You know what I meant."

Nichole laughed. "Let's get breakfast. What's on the menu today? Something smells amazing."

"It's quiche for the main course plus a whole compliment of side dishes. You know how Emmit is about having a wide selection to choose from."

"Yep."

"Nobody leaves hungry," they said in unison, and both burst out laughing.

"Exactly."

They ate outside, enjoying the cool temperature and the even better company. By the time they finished, they had to leave for her appointment. The ride wasn't very long, which only disturbed Nichole even more.

"What's wrong? You've been awfully quiet this morning." Mark split his attention between the road and Nichole. They came to a red stoplight, and he turned to catch her full attention. He reached over and took her hand, squeezing it to encourage her to talk.

"I'm worried." She glanced at Mark before looking back out the windshield.

"Your knee seems to be much better; you hardly limp anymore. Why are you worried?"

Her throat closed up, and her breath hitched.

"Hey, Nichole, you can talk to me about anything. You know that, right?"

Unbidden, a tear dropped from her eye. "I know. I'm just scared that as soon as I don't need your help anymore that you'll leave me. We're running out of excuses and time to be together. In another couple of days, you'll head back to Atlanta to start flying again. And I've got my dad to look after." She sniffled, hating how weak and silly she sounded.

"I don't want things to change. I like what we've created together. Does that make me selfish?"

"Terribly!" He practically growled out the word.

She couldn't believe he'd agree with her so readily. Had she been that bad? "What?"

He laughed. "You should see the look on your face. Look, Nichole, if you've been selfish, then I've been doubly so. Here I am freeloading at your house. I haven't once wanted to leave, so that makes me the selfish one, not you. I don't have to go back to Atlanta. Not right away, at least."

"But what about your job?" She loved hearing him say he'd stay, but not if it meant he'd lose everything.

"It can wait. I've got vacation time saved up."

"Don't you miss flying?"

"I'd miss you more. Besides, I could fly anytime. And, I could do something other than flying. I'm pretty versatile in my skillset."

"Oh, yes. I forgot about you being Mr. NFL and all. But I wouldn't ask you to give up what you love doing. I already know what that feels like, and I wouldn't wish it on my worst enemy."

"You worry too much, Nichole. I promise that everything will work out exactly as it should. Trust me, okay?"

She wanted desperately to believe him. If only she could freeze time and keep things as they were right now. "I was thinking about asking Dr. Benson about genetic testing. You were right that I should find out where I stand."

"Sounds like a wise decision. Maybe we should have a special dinner tonight to celebrate."

"Sounds like a stretch, but I'm game."

"Great. Let's dress up and make it into a real affair."

"I've gotten pretty used to seeing you in a tee shirt and jeans." She didn't add that she thought he looked pretty sexy in that attire. "I'd like to see how you clean up. It's a date!"

CHAPTER 19

MARKSON

Markson stepped out of the shower with one towel wrapped around his hips and another in his hand to rub over his hair. His nerves made him shaky, but his excitement kept him moving. Tonight, his whole life would take a new course.

He dropped the second towel into the laundry basket as he entered the bedroom. He had his suit laid out on the bed, wrinkle-free and ready for him to put on. The black case holding Nichole's engagement ring sat prominently on his nightstand. Sitting next to the suit, Markson picked up the velvet box and cracked open the lid.

The four-carat diamond solitaire flashed sparkles of light in every direction. He could already envision it on Nichole's elegant hand. In under an hour, he'd ask her the most important question of both of their lives.

Annoyingly, his cell phone rang. He thought about ignoring it, imagining it was another work issue. He couldn't see who was calling since the phone rested on the dresser beside the door. Getting up, he glanced at the screen and saw Stephen's name displayed. That was odd. Stephen only seldom called; he wasn't one for idle conversation.

He swiped to answer the call and immediately put it on speaker so he could dress at the same time. "Hey, Stephen."

"Dude! Oh, thank goodness you picked up. I've tried calling you like six times in the last twenty minutes. Where've you been?"

He retraced his steps and set the phone on the bed. "I was in the shower. What's wrong, Stephen? You know you can tell me anything." Markson had never heard Stephen sound so strange. Whatever was going on, it wasn't good. The second towel fell into a heap at his feet, and he pulled on his boxers.

The noise of Stephen clearing his throat echoed through the quiet room. "How serious are you about Nichole?"

That had to be a rhetorical question, which wasn't like Stephen at all. "What are you talking about? You know I already bought her an engagement ring. I'm planning to propose to her tonight." He picked up the box and admired the ring again.

He grabbed the dress pants from the bed and put one leg in. "What's going on? Did you discover something from her past that you think will change my mind? I'm telling you right now, no matter what you think she's done, I don't care." He'd never been so acutely aware of the sound a zipper made.

Stephen's prolonged silence made Markson worry.

"This might change your mind."

Markson didn't have time to play word games, and it wasn't like Stephen to be melodramatic. The sooner he knew the problem, the faster he could resolve the issue. "Would you spit it out already? I've got to get ready for dinner."

"You can't marry Nichole. She's your first cousin. Her mother was your mother's sister."

Time seemed to stop. Markson's field of vision narrowed to a single spot of lint resting on the dresser in front of him. He had to have heard Stephen wrong. If he and Nichole were related, he would have known about it long before now. "That's not right, man. I think you've got her mixed up with someone else."

"I'm telling you the truth. I checked and rechecked the records a dozen times. Do you think I wanted this to be true? I've heard how you talk about Nichole, and it's killing me to have to tell you."

"I don't know what to say." That put it mildly; his mind couldn't process how this could have happened.

"I'll keep searching the records. If I discover anything else, I'll let you know. Again, I'm really sorry, Markson."

The phone screen went blank since Stephen hung up. Thankfully, Markson was already seated on the bed. His legs felt as numb as the rest of his body. He trusted Stephen implicitly, but there had to be a mistake.

He would have known if his mother's sister had a child. Wouldn't he? But his mother never talked about her sister—not after the falling out they'd had.

What was the likelihood that they'd meet in Atlanta? If only Nichole's mother were still alive to get answers. She might not be, but there was still Jacob. Surely, he knew something to clear up this misunderstanding.

NICHOLE

"I'm going to do some research on that company, Dad. Maybe if I talk to someone in charge, they'll agree to rescind the contract once they hear what Sal did." Nichole would have done this days before, but Mark had kept her so busy she never seemed to find the time. Jacob rolled his eyes and dismissively waved as he left the room.

Months ago, when she first found out about the theft, she'd heard the name wrong. It was no wonder her previous internet searches had returned without any information. At the time, she'd thought it was a fake company name designed to steal businesses.

With Mark making business calls and taking a shower, she would get this taken care of. Maybe she was trying to distract herself. Mark wasn't acting like himself ever since she caught him and her father talking this morning. Was he thanking her father for letting him stay?

Tonight's dinner might be his way of saying goodbye. She didn't want to think he'd do that to her, but why else would he suddenly want to have a fancy dinner?

After talking with her dad tonight, she finally had the actual company name. Dragging her father's laptop over onto her lap, she typed in the correct name and waited for the slow internet connection to pull up the search results. She clicked on the home page, expecting to see some shady-looking site, but that's not what pulled up. This looked for all the world like a reputable, prosperous company.

She clicked over to the About Us page and read the blurb about it being a company that respected its investors and worked with the communities to make everyone prosperous. Growling in disgust, she shook her head. "Yeah, you sure make it sound like you care. But that's not at all what really happens."

She'd seen enough to know this company wanted to paint a better picture than the reality they left in their wake. She clicked the Contact Us page and started writing her complaint letter. Paragraphs flowed from her fingers onto the page, outlining all of her grievances and pleas for help.

It felt good to get all of that off of her chest finally. She thought about asking her dad to read it as well but then decided against it. If he told her to delete the message, then she'd feel obligated to comply.

No, this message had to go to the company so they could know what happened. What if they had a disreputable agent working for them? That was a vague possibility; it made her feel better to give them the benefit of the doubt.

In fact, it would be even better if she sent it directly to the owner rather than to some office flunky who'd probably disregard it anyway. She opened another tab on her browser and pulled up the company website again. This time, she clicked on the "Employee Directory" page.

The list was in alphabetical order and included individual names and email addresses on the left and the employee's picture on the right. She'd hit the jackpot. Not only could she visualize who she was making a personal plea to, but she could also direct her message to him or her: no middle man, no run-around.

She scrolled, confident that she could get this mess resolved even faster now. Finally, there he was: Markson Rothschild, President. Her eyes flicked over to the picture, ready to hate him on sight, knowing he had to be an old miserly scrooge. The face staring back at her was Mark's. Her Mark. The same Mark who was getting dressed for dinner in the other room.

No. There had to be some mistake. Mark was a corporate pilot. He wasn't a billionaire who preyed on innocent people. Not her Mark.

Scrambling to her feet, her computer balanced on her forearm, she almost ran through the house and burst into Mark's bedroom. "Tell me this isn't true, Mark. Tell me you haven't been lying to me this whole time."

"We have to talk, Nichole. You're not going to like what I have to say." Mark grabbed her elbow and spun her around.

He marched her out of his room, his fingers digging painfully into her arm.

"I don't hear you denying anything. Mark, or should I call you Markson, since that's your real name?"

"Where's Jacob?"

It was so aggravating how he ignored her questions as if they didn't matter. What was wrong with him?

Nichole tried to pull her arm away, but it was useless. She attempted to stop walking, only to be drug along helplessly. Rather than waste her energy fighting against his evident strength, she walked faster, forcing him to keep up with her. She was not going to be his victim again. Not anymore. He was going to answer her questions.

They burst into Jacob's office almost side by side. His smile faded as he looked from his daughter to Markson. "Did you ever ask Mark his full name, Dad?"

"No. Did you?" Jacob frowned, turning his gaze over to Nichole.

She paused to consider. "No, I didn't, but the nurse at the hospital said he'd filled out his paperwork as Mark Roth. But that's not his name. Dad, look here." She plonked the laptop onto his desk and turned it until her father could see the screen. Leaning forward, she pointed to the picture and said,

"His real name is Markson Rothschild of Rothschild Venture Capitalist. He's the one who stole your company. He's been here spying on us and doing who knows what else."

"Now wait a minute—," Markson began but paused when Jacob held up his hand to stop him.

"Mark, or Markson, hasn't been here spying, Nichole. You're getting too excited. Sit down, both of you. We have to clear the air before things get out of control."

Markson sat and quirked his eyebrow challengingly when Nichole hesitated.

She knew better than to cross her father when he spoke with such authority. She pulled her chair farther from Markson's before she dropped gracelessly into it. The twinge of pain reminded her to be more careful, but her mind still raged at Markson's deception.

Markson perched himself on the edge of the chair. "Sir, if I may." After receiving a nod of approval, he continued. "I just received information from my friend, Stephen, that there's a situation that I'd like to get clarification on."

"Go ahead. I'm listening."

After a long sigh, he said, "Did Shannon have a sister?"

"What? Who cares, Markson? Why are you changing the subject?" Nichole glared at him, wishing he'd just leave so they could have their peaceful life back. The way Markson wouldn't even look at her only infuriated her further.

Likewise, Jacob ignored the outburst and nodded. "Yes. I think her name was Sheryl. No, that's not right. Ferrell, maybe?" He drummed his fingers loudly against the desktop.

"Was it Ferriel Clayton?"

"Yes. That's it. What does that mean to you?"

"Jacob, that's my mother. I think I should go. My mom needs to know that her sister's gone. Do you think you could go to the airport with me? You can bring my car back here; it's already in Nichole's name."

Nichole tried to wrap her mind around what Markson was saying. "Wait, are you implying that you and I are cousins? Like, first cousins?" She recoiled in horror, remembering how she'd told him that she loved him and wanted to marry him.

Not only was he a deceitful, stealing crook, but he was also related to her. They'd never be able to forget he existed. And she would never forget how she felt when she kissed him.

CHAPTER 20
MARKSON

Markson woodenly stood and left Jacob's office. Numbly, he packed everything he'd accumulated into the suitcase the courier had brought for him. Jacob had confirmed everything that Stephen had discovered. It was the worst possible outcome, but probably the best possible time.

He looked over at the black velvet box on the nightstand. He didn't want to take it with him. If he left it there, maybe Nichole or Jacob could sell it. At least someone would get some benefit out of it.

Before leaving his room, he texted Jenkins. ***I hope you're nearby. Rotor up within the hour.***

Wheeling his suitcase behind him, he grabbed his work satchel and slung the strap over his shoulder. Jacob met him at the front door, neither of them feeling the need to speak, but Markson could imagine what he was thinking of him.

Jacob's pitying look would haunt him forever. But, knowing he'd hurt Nichole made everything ten times worse. Markson threw his bags into the back seat of the SUV before getting into the driver's seat.

The ride was painfully quiet. Markson wanted to apologize, but he didn't have the words to say. Was he sorry? Only for keeping the truth from Jacob. He could have told him and had everything be better. But none of that would have changed the outcome. He couldn't change his mother's identity.

Markson pulled into the parking space at the airport. He sighed, still looking straight ahead. Nodding to himself, he reached for his satchel and pulled it into his lap. Rifling through the contents, he pulled out a folder and held it out to Jacob. "This is yours."

"What is it?" Jacob's hands automatically took the folder, but his eyes remained fixed on Markson.

"It's the paperwork reverting your company to your ownership. I put my team on this the moment I discovered the fraud perpetrated by Sal. You can see the date stamps. My intern handled this purchase, and I honestly didn't know that you were unaware of the sale. I first heard about it when Nichole was flying here with me."

"Strange how fate brought the two of you together," Jacob mused quietly. "Thank you for doing this, Markson. After all of the help you gave in finding Sal, I knew you weren't the deceptive sort. Sal may have fooled me, but I'm certain you are exactly as you've been since I've known you."

Markson pulled out another folder and passed it to Jacob. "This is the deed to the Smythe's house. I bought it for Nichole while we were still in the hospital. It's already in her name. Same as this SUV, as I told you in your office."

Jacob said, "You really love her, don't you?"

"It doesn't matter now. Besides, I doubt she'll forgive me for keeping my identity a secret."

"I'm curious why you did, too. You could have told me the truth."

Breathing heavily through his nose, he turned and stared at Jacob for several seconds. "I know. It's a defense mechanism I've learned to use. I don't use my real name when I'm traveling. You'd be surprised how many people try to do crazy things when they learn about my money. I didn't try to deceive Nichole."

He sighed again. "That's not entirely true. She was so mad at my company because of that deal."

He pointed to the folder in Jacob's lap. "I didn't think she'd grow to love me if she knew the truth of who I was before getting to know me.

"It sounds stupid when I say it out loud. I'm really sorry, Jacob. I should have been honest with both of you from the moment I knew who you were. Maybe things would have turned out better. But, as I said, it doesn't change the reality of the situation between Nichole and me. We're still related.

"I hope she doesn't hate me forever. Someday, I'd like to get back in touch. I don't have too many extended relatives. It's a shame that this all turned out as it did." He turned to look out the windshield. "Ah, there's my pilot. Thanks again, Jacob. You've been wonderful, and I'm glad I got to know you. Tell Nichole how sorry I am. Maybe she'll forgive me."

⇥⇥⇥ ⇤⇤⇤

How could he still feel so conflicted about Nichole? Even a week later, his heart always wanted to be with her, but his mind told him to let her go. He couldn't have the scandal of marrying his first cousin.

The memory of telling his mom about her long-lost sister made him cringe. Everyone in the family knew about his mom and her sister's fallout when they were only teenagers.

Nobody had heard from Shannon ever again. But, Markson was sure that nobody wanted her dead.

Even pouring himself back into work did little to distract his thoughts from reverting to Nichole. As he'd promised, he worked twelve to fourteen hours every day reviewing every purchase he hadn't personally handled. Luckily, none of them had any issues.

He closed the file on the last contract. Everyone had already gone home to their families for the evening, leaving him alone in his misery. Nobody could ever replace Nichole in his heart. He'd never have anyone to go home to at night.

His cell phone rang.

He ignored it.

It wouldn't matter if a world leader wanted to give him the deal of a lifetime; he wanted to feel what he'd had with Nichole again.

The second time his office phone rang, he grabbed the receiver and slapped it down again.

Maybe whoever kept calling would get the message that he didn't want to talk. If he couldn't have any peace in his office, perhaps he should go for a walk.

Grabbing his cell phone, he put it on 'do not disturb' mode and shoved it in his pocket. Now, the only people who could reach him would be those on his contact list—a very short list consisting of his five college friends.

He hadn't made it out of the building before his phone vibrated with an incoming message followed almost immediately by it ringing.

"Oh, for Pete's sake!" he said, pulling the phone from his pocket and swiping it to answer without even looking to see the caller's name. "What?!"

"Someone's not having a good day. It's a good thing I called."

"Listen, Stephen; I'm not in the mood for this. Whatever it is will have to wait. I've had a long day." His hand clenched the phone so hard it pulled on his newly healed skin across his palm. At least the pain distracted him from how his broken heart felt.

"It's about Nichole."

His pulse raced. What if something happened to her? Did he need to do something to help her? "Is she okay?"

"What? I don't know."

Relief and frustration rushed through him. "Jeez, Stephen. Don't do that to me."

"I sent you the documents via text, email, fax, and courier. You may want to check out on life, but I've been busy over here. No matter how hard you tried to avoid me, I was going to fulfill my promise."

"What are you talking about? I didn't get anything. When did all of this happen?" He jogged through the lobby and angrily pushed through the main door, almost hitting the man outside, reaching for the handle.

"I have a personal delivery for Markson Rothschild," the man said.

Either he was too distracted or dumbfounded, but he automatically answered, "That's me."

The man held out an envelope and a clipboard. "Sign here."

Markson juggled to hold the cell phone up to his ear with his shoulder while he took the package and signed for it. "Thanks."

Stephen said, "See. Courier. Right on time, too. My work is done for the night. I suggest you read what I found tonight. You can thank me later."

No goodbyes were necessary. The call ended, and Markson shoved his phone back into his pocket.

Turning on his heel, he opened the door and locked it behind him. "This better be good, Stephen," he grumbled.

His heart raced.

Stephen was too good of a friend to yank his chain. Whatever he held in his hands was going to be important. Especially important since he knew it had to do with Nichole.

Back at his desk, he didn't make a single sound as he poured over the documents. This had to be the most incredible story ever told. They made movies out of stuff not even this convoluted.

There was only one thing he could do with this information. But he couldn't do it alone.

Grabbing his phone, he sent a text: ***Get the jet ready for flight. I'm taking a trip tonight.***

Even the thrill of flying his new plane for the first time could not compare with what he planned.

CHAPTER 21

NICHOLE

"Nichole, I think we need to talk," Jacob said where he stood in her bedroom doorway. "Come out to the living room." He didn't wait to see if she would refuse; he turned and walked away.

Something about the way his shoulders sagged alarmed Nichole.

She set down the ring box on her nightstand and wiped the tear from her cheek. It was impossible not to cry when she thought about the life she'd mentally planned with Mark. Finding the ring had just about broken her resolve to hate him, but some things were unforgivable.

She stepped carefully, preserving the progress she'd made with her knee. In only a few more days, she'd be able to resume her usual activities.

"I don't want to hear you trying to defend Markson again. He lied, Dad. He lied to both of us, and I can't believe you're not more upset about this."

"I don't want to talk about Markson, Nichole." He kept walking until he reached his favorite chair in the living room.

He looked older than she'd ever seen him before. "I want to talk about your mother. Sit down and listen." He didn't watch her progress; he stared at the low flames in the fireplace.

Why would he suddenly want to talk about her mom? At any other time, she would have been thrilled with this change of heart, but today it scared her. Something about his voice made her want to run back into her room and hide from whatever he was about to reveal.

"Dad, it's okay. We don't have to do this right now." Her heart raced, she felt like something terrible was about to happen, something she had thought about for all of her life, but she tried her best to ignore it.

"You're wrong. I've already waited too long to tell you. I should have told you the truth years ago, but your mother made me promise I wouldn't say anything unless it became absolutely necessary."

"Dad, you're scaring me. What are you talking about?" She collapsed on the couch, her legs felt rubbery, and her hands were cold and shaking.

"You've known your whole life that I wasn't your father, but you accepted me anyway. I hope you'll still love me the same after I'm done."

"Done with what, Dad? Stop being cryptic and just spit it out."

"Your mother had M.S., and she knew it would be impossible for her to have a child of her own."

"Dad, it's okay. Mom already told me the story about how I was her miracle. This isn't a secret. Jeez, you were scaring me." She exhaled, feeling better already until her Dad spoke.

"Yes, you were a miracle, but not because she gave birth to you. The miracle was that you survived. Let me start from the beginning. Promise me that you'll listen and not interrupt."

"Okay. I promise." She hadn't heard anything about any health scares as an infant. Her medical records hadn't mentioned anything unusual, either.

"You were born healthy and happy. Both of your parents loved and adored you. They'd been planning for your arrival for many years but never thought they'd have a child of their own. After the fourth round of in-vitro fertilization, they discovered they were finally pregnant.

"When you were three months old, your parents decided to take you home to meet your grandparents. They booked a private airplane because it was more convenient than taking a commercial flight since they had to go to the small town where your grandparents lived. This turned out to be a grave mistake.

"An hour into the flight, the pilot had a heart attack and died. Neither of your parents knew how to fly and were helpless to stop the airplane from crashing. Everyone on board died—everyone, that is, except you. The official report said that your car seat saved your life.

"Shannon was receiving an M.S. treatment at the hospital when they brought you in. She recognized you immediately because she was your godmother. You could imagine how distraught she became when she found out her best friend had died. She moved heaven and earth to adopt you and raise you as her child.

"We were engaged when she started the adoption process. Her attorney said she'd have an easier time adopting if she were married. So, we got married, and the adoption went through under her name only.

"You were three when I legally adopted you, but I didn't change your name. Your mother always wanted you to keep your real name to honor her best friend. It became apparent that Shannon's health was failing; I couldn't stand the idea of losing both of you.

"So, now you know everything. I hope you can forgive me for keeping this from you."

She looked at the man she'd called dad as if she didn't even know who he was anymore. Everything about her life had been a lie. Everybody who she thought loved her had lied to her. Was she such a horrible person that nobody felt they needed to be truthful with her?

Rather than say something she'd regret, she stood and left the room. Spots swam in her vision as she fought to get enough air in her lungs. Her erratic heartbeats pulsed down to her fingertips, which contrasted wildly with how numb she felt inside.

"Nichole! Please talk to me."

She didn't pause or even acknowledge the sorrowful cry of the man she'd called dad. Without any conscious decision, she found herself inside the one room that always reminded her of her mother. Her dad had put all of her mother's favorite things in this room because he missed her, too. "My adoptive mother," she whispered. "She's not my mom. My real parents are dead."

Her laughter sounded hollow in the sunny room. She no longer felt any connection to her mother here. She didn't even know her mother.

Had her adoptive mother told her the truth about who her birth father had been? Did her stepdad know? What else had they kept from her?

Falling to her knees, she barely noticed the feel of someone's hand on her shoulder. She should have shrugged it off, but she needed someone to hold her before she fell to pieces.

With her eyes still closed and her heart breaking, she turned and threw her arms around him. He always knew how to comfort her.

When she drew in a shaky breath, she knew the truth about the man who held her so tightly. He loved her.

"Why are you here?" She cried harder, wishing this could be real.

Maybe her mind had cracked. She didn't want to lose this feeling. Somehow Markson had changed his mind about her and had come to sweep her off her feet. He would tell her everything was okay.

"We aren't related, Nichole. Stephen found the proof. I came as soon as I found out. Nichole, honey! What's wrong? Who hurt you?"

Nichole stiffened as she realized this wasn't a figment of her imagination. Markson *was* here. Somehow he knew exactly the right time to be here for her.

She pushed herself away, falling onto her rear at the same time as her eyes snapped open to see Markson. "How? How are you here?"

"I just told you. I came here to talk to you, and your dad practically shoved me down the hall and into this room. Are you going to tell me what happened to make you so upset?"

"He's not my dad. I don't know who he is or who I am, for that matter."

"I know he's not your dad. You told me he's your stepdad."

Nichole smeared her palms against her cheeks to wipe away all of the tears. She had to get a hold of herself and start making sense of what everyone was telling her. It wasn't as if she were a fragile girl. Her dad had raised her to be self-sufficient.

Her dad. Yes. He was her dad in every way that mattered. And she'd walked out on him and left him hurting. "I have to talk to my dad. Excuse me."

She pushed herself up from the floor and stumbled across the room. She had to make this right, or else she'd never forgive herself.

"I'm coming with you." He grabbed her hand as she passed.

She curled her fingers around his strong palm, knowing he had to stay with her. Ever since they met, they were in this together. As unlikely as it sounded, a plane crash had brought her to Markson's aunt, and then a plane crash had brought her to Markson.

Fate had linked them together, and she meant to see where this would go.

CHAPTER 22
NICHOLE

"So, who were my birth parents?" Nichole asked her dad. As unreal as it seemed to have Markson sitting beside her on the couch, she was thankful to have his support. Her fingers nearly crushed his with how hard she held onto him, but he didn't seem to notice or care.

Jacob cleared his throat. "Sophie and Greg Childress. Sophie was the first person Shannon befriended when she moved here. They were inseparable. I think they bonded because of Sophie's difficulty in getting pregnant. Shannon was living vicariously through her best friend's struggles, cheering her on and supporting her emotionally whenever the procedures failed to produce a pregnancy."

"Well, at least she told me my father's real name. There's that, I guess. I don't know why it had to be such a big secret. Adopted kids grow up knowing the truth all the time, and they turn out fine." Nichole looked from her dad to Markson, trying to see any agreement.

Both of them nodded.

"It was your mother's dying wish, Nichole. She knew the truth would hurt you, and she wanted to save you from that pain. Plus, I think she wanted to believe that you were her child. Maybe the medication made her forget that she didn't birth you. Who knows? But she loved you until her dying day. Your name was the last word she ever spoke."

"You never told me that, Dad." She brushed another tear away. "So, my parents died, but they were going to visit my grandparents. Are they still alive?"

"No. They died a couple of years after your parents. Greg's parents both died before you were born. I'm afraid your extended family isn't going to get any bigger with this news. I'm sorry."

"That's not true. Shannon might not have been Nichole's real mom, but she was my aunt. It may seem strange at first, but my parents would like to meet you. I don't have to be there if my presence would make you uncomfortable.

"I really made a mess of things between us, but I never wanted to hurt you. I hope you believe me." Markson's hand squeezed hers as if trying to compel her to agree.

"I think that's my cue to leave," Jacob announced.

Nichole didn't even have a chance to respond before her dad practically ran from the room.

Her head was spinning. Was any of this true? How could Markson be sitting here listening to her dad's fantastic tale?

Any minute she'd wake up and find herself panting and sweating in bed from the nightmare.

Pulling her hand free, she reached over and pinched herself. "Ouch!"

"What are you doing?"

"Seeing if I'm dreaming. You can't feel pain in a dream. Right?"

"Do you still think you're dreaming?"

"I don't know. Maybe. I must be because, in reality, I'm furious at you. Right now, I can't remember being happier to have you with me."

"Well, then maybe this will convince you that this is your new reality." Markson pulled her close, pausing for only a split second to say, "I love you, Nichole."

His lips crushed against hers, and she felt herself respond in kind.

If this were a dream, then she didn't want to wake up. In this reality, she could have everything, and nobody could say anything against it. She wanted that for herself.

She wanted Markson, even if he were a billionaire.

That last qualification made her giggle. She couldn't keep kissing Markson and pulled back. "I'm sorry. I think I'm losing it. All of this is real. Wait, did you say that Stephen told you the truth?"

"Yes, but I didn't know if you knew the truth. Jacob didn't tell me anything before he yanked me inside and took me to you. It wasn't my place to tell you, but I was going to force Jacob to admit the truth. I wasn't going to let a lie keep us apart."

"That's funny. It wasn't even that lie that made me mad. But all of that is stupid to dwell on now. I think we both know that life is too short to let misunderstandings go unresolved.

"Dad tried to fix things, but I was too stubborn to listen. I want to thank you for giving him back his company."

"Yeah, you can't imagine how sick I felt when you told me his company's name. But I wanted to get to the bottom of it before I said anything. I should have spoken up right then. I'm sorry."

"Hey, I get it. You didn't know me, and I could have been lying. It could've been a case of seller's remorse. You had to investigate."

"I love you."

"I love you, too. That's never going to get old. Oh, I found the ring in your old bedroom. It's stunning. Was that supposed to be the special dinner celebration surprise?"

"Yes, before everything blew up. Do you still have it?"

"Yes. It's in my room. Do you want it?"

"Maybe. Will you get it, please?"

She couldn't help but feel a little hurt that he'd take it back. When she reached the hallway, she heard Markson call out behind her.

"Ask Jacob to come back with you. There's something I want to share with both of you."

Nichole brought her dad back with her. They entered the living room to find Markson standing in front of the fireplace, hand resting on the mantle, with his head bowed.

"Here it is," she said, tapping him on the shoulder.

"Thank you." He took the little box and cracked it open to reveal the ring inside. "It's just as beautiful as you, Nichole."

He dropped to one knee and held the box in front of him. "Nichole, we've had a rough start, but I promise only sunshine and roses are in our future. I love you and only ever want to have you at my side. Will you marry me?"

Nichole pinched herself again. The pain didn't cause the tears in her eyes. She grabbed at Markson's hands to get him up from the floor. "A hundred times, YES!"

Through her tears, she loved seeing Markson's sexy smile. He stepped closer, grabbed her hand, and slipped the ring on her finger.

"It's official. As soon as you set the date, you'll be Mrs. Nichole Rothschild. You've made me the happiest man alive. I love you so much!"

Sparks flew as soon as his lips touched hers. She'd never known how much she could love someone until that moment. It meant so much more because she almost missed this perfect match. Never again. He was her forever.

⤜⟫⟫⟩ ⟨⟨⟨⟪⤛

"We still have the same problem about having children," Nichole said. "The only difference is you're the potential carrier rather than me."

"I thought you'd say that. I researched, and M.S.'s inheritance pattern is unknown even though it appears to be passed down through families. Because Shannon was my aunt, I had my DNA analyzed, and I don't have the three so-called "complement system" genes that play a role in MS-caused vision loss. We can have children, Nichole. Or we can adopt. I'm up for either or both; it doesn't matter to me.

"Wow, I thought you just found out about my real past. Why did you have the tests done?"

Markson shrugged. "For the same reason I thought you should do it—peace of mind. Now, I'm doubly glad I had it done so you won't have to worry. It never hurts to be prepared for the future."

"Hmm. What else have you planned for my life?"

"Just you wait! I promise you'll never get bored." Markson planted his lips on hers, sealing his promise with a kiss.

Epilogue

(Six Months Later) – Markson

"We could have gone anywhere in the world, but when I thought about what would make you happiest, I knew it wasn't going to be a tropical beach somewhere. Okay, we're almost there; just a couple more steps, and then you can take off your blindfold." Markson's face hurt from smiling so long. He knew this was the perfect wedding gift for Nichole, even though it was three months late. "Ready?"

"Beyond ready. Can I look now?" Nichole's feet shifted, and her hands rose to her blindfold in anticipation of her husband's response.

"Yes."

The silken fabric quickly slipped from her head, fluttering away in the breeze as Nichole's fingers forgot to hold it. "Is this a treehouse?" Her mouth dropped open, and her eyes tried to take in every detail at once. She turned to Markson. "Is this the project you were working on when we first met?"

"The same one. I didn't know what it would mean at the time, but when I finally traveled out here, I knew this was exactly what you'd love to have. I had the builder put in everything you love. Just wait until you see the inside."

Nichole turned away, admiring the view. "I thought this was supposed to be a subdivision. And where's the road?"

"Most of the parcels are an acre. This one is on five acres. We have houses all around us, but the builder was careful to camouflage them from one another to keep the setting as natural as possible. If you look down there," he pointed beyond where their Rolls-Royce Phantom was parked, "that green strip is the road. They used a special ground cover and bioluminescence for the road's lines. As I said, they thought of everything to keep this as green as possible. Come inside. I have another surprise for you."

"What else could there be? This place is already more than enough. You already gave me the best wedding present when you gave my dad back his company. I don't need anything."

"That's where you're wrong. You deserve this and so much more."

He'd spend the rest of his life thinking of things to give her. No amount of money could ever show her how much he loved her.

His hand rested on the small of her back as he led her up the rocking wood bridge to the treehouse entrance.

Once he opened the front door, he let her wander through the great room and kitchen. He waited for her to notice the view, and it didn't take long. It was one of the reasons he'd bought this particular plot.

"There's a stream running over there. Do you see that?" She turned, her eyes wide with delight.

"Yes. It was the reason I bought you here. It reminded me of our first day together."

Nichole took his hand in hers. Her fingertips traced the N-shaped scar on his palm. He liked teasing her that she'd branded him from the moment they met.

His fingers curled around her hand. Leading her across the living room, he said, "Your surprise is right over here."

"What is it?"

"If I told you, then it wouldn't be a surprise." He opened the door and led her inside.

"It's a nursery. How did you know?"

Markson pulled Nichole into his arms, overwhelmed with emotion. "I didn't know, but I hoped. We're going to be the perfect family, Nichole. I love you."

She turned her face up toward his. Her lips parted ever so slightly, inviting him to come closer.

He leaned down; his love almost overwhelmed him. This was his wife, the mother of his future children.

He had no idea how he'd managed to get so lucky to find Nichole, but he was going to make every day memorable for her. She deserved it.

His lips touched hers, and he was lost for eternity. His love expanded with every moment he spent with Nichole. She was his everything.

She pulled away, stopping inches from him and looking into his eyes. "Do you know what this baby will mean?"

"Other than I'll get to call you mommy?" He loved hearing how that sounded.

"Yes, other than that, Daddy. I won't be able to spend much time as your Project Manager. This little bundle of joy will take priority. You'll probably have to hire someone else to take my place."

"Nobody could ever take your place."

"You know what I mean."

"I do. We'll worry about that when the time comes. I'll even let you hire your replacement."

"You're too kind." Nichole turned, still holding herself tight to his side. Her gaze swept over the whole room; tears glistened as she looked back up at her husband.

"It's going to be an amazing adventure. Don't you think?" He'd never seen eyes as beautiful as hers. Hopefully, their children would inherit them from her.

"Yes. And I'm glad I get to do it with you."

"I agree." He took her hand so they could walk through their summer home together. They stepped outside to admire the view from the back deck.

Nichole inhaled the fresh air. She looked content. Suddenly, she frowned as something crossed her mind. "Did you ever thank Stephen for his part in getting us back together?"

"Yep."

"We should give him a gift."

"I already did."

"You gave him something already? What was it?"

"Five million dollars."

Nichole laughed. "Seriously. What did you give him?"

"I am serious. That's how much money I cost him by marrying you first. I thought it was only fair to repay him."

Nichole slowly shook her head. "Ah, yes. The old college pact."

Markson pulled his wife close to his chest, his chin resting on the top of her head as he said, "Besides, I think *you* are the best investment I've ever made. We make the perfect team. Our children will have the best parents in the whole world."

The End...For Now

Continue the series with An Unleashed Love, Book 6, in the Billionaire's Bet Romances

Get My Free Book Now

To let others know how much you enjoyed this book, please leave a review at your favorite retailer.

To keep updated on upcoming books, visit www.amyproebstel.com.

Receive a FREE prequel story,

A Billionaire's Patent for Love

by signing up for Amy Proebstel's newsletter.

You can also follow Amy Proebstel on Facebook at www.facebook.com/ATwistOnReality.

About the Author

Amy is a *USA Today* bestselling author who writes sweet romance and young adult medical romance.

When she's not busy writing about endearing heroes, scheming villains, and Lone Star love stories, she spends her time binge-watching Hallmark movies, taking her husband and daughter flying (but not in the jets her billionaire's fly), playing with her Pomeranian and Pomskies, and cats, or reading.

A.B. Proebstel is the sweet romance pen name for Amy Proebstel, who also writes progression fantasy, epic dragon fantasy, and paranormal romance books that add a little magic to the world.

Please sign up for Amy's fantasy or romance newsletters on

her website at www.AmyProebstel.com or click Follow on her bio to get notices and updates when she releases new books!

- Get a bonus scene from A Cowboy's Recipe for Romance: https://geni.us/B1-ACRFR-Bonus

- Join her mailing list: https://geni.us/CleanRomance

- Join her Facebook group: facebook.com/ATwistOnReality

- Visit her website: amyproebstel.com

- Follow her on X: https://geni.us/Amy-T

- Follow her on Instagram: instagram.com/amyproebstel

She loves hearing from her readers.

Also By
Amy Proebstel

Billionaire's Bet, A Sweet Romance Series

Sweet Creek Ranch, A Sweet Romance Series

Wolf Shifters of Catskill County, A Clean Fated Mate Shifter Series

The Chosen, A Fantasy & Magic Adventure Series

Dragon's Magic: An Epic Dragon Fantasy Series

The Rift in Our Reality, A Sweet Young Adult Medical Romance

9 781946 292407